MUSAWI

ISRAEL BOOKSHOP
PUBLICATIONS

MUSAWI

a novel

A. Shalom

Cover design by: Miriam Isaac

Published by:
Israel Bookshop Publications
501 Prospect Street
Lakewood, NJ 08701

Tel: (732) 901-3009
Fax: (732) 901-4012
www.israelbookshoppublications.com
info@israelbookshoppublications.com

Printed in Canada

To my grandparents

Yosef (Tofic) and Shefiah Cohen a"h

who inspired me to write this story.

To all of our ancestors

who continue to inspire us each day.

Acknowledgments_____

I would like to thank the many people who helped turn this story into a novel. To the professional staff of Israel Bookshop Publications, it has been a pleasure working with each one of you. To Mr. Moshe Kaufman for his acceptance of this story and hands-on involvement through each stage of this work. To Mrs. Liron Delmar, for her dedication and efficiency. To Mrs. Malkie Gendelman for her expert editing. To Mrs. Adina Lover for her detailed proofreading. To M. Isaac for her extraordinary cover design.

To the invaluable eyewitnesses who were able to explain the many mysteries of life in Damascus and Syria no matter how many times I called: Mrs. Dolly Basala, Mrs. Julie Levi, Mrs. Sillia Halawani, Mrs. Violet Galapo, Mr. Zaki Jarada, Mrs. Rita Safdieh, Dr. Benny Zalta, and Mrs. Janet Zalta.

To Dr. Nathan Ades for his medical expertise.

To Joan for her thorough critiques again and again.

A special thank you to Rabbi Isaac Dwek, Rabbi Gavriel Finkel, Rabbi Michael Malka, Rabbi Edmond Nahum, and Rabbi Chaim Aharon Weinberg who helped me in many ways with this novel.

To my family, my lifeline, whose love and support I live on.

Above all, my gratitude and appreciation belongs to Hashem *Yitbarach* as everything is fashioned through His Benevolence.

1

Shrill screams blasted through the quiet stares and soft chatter that blanketed the Jewish Quarter of Damascus. Some people stopped what they were doing. Others turned toward the commotion. Few went straight toward the noises, as most people tried to avoid the possibility of incriminating themselves by the mere acknowledgement of what was going on.

The screams winded down several narrow streets before they reached her.

Sophia stopped instantly. She grabbed her sister Boomeh. Side by side, they squeezed into a shop selling herbs and flowers.

Sophia peered through the window display.

"What are you doing? Come inside." Boomeh inched as far away from the doorway as she could. Sophia didn't budge. The screams of the unseen person stopped, but a sharp ear could hear the yelling and praying continuing as the commotion traveled farther and farther away.

Inside the shop, an Arab man placed down the receiver of the telephone. Sophia stared at the telephone, the one privilege which Jews in Damascus were unable to have. She looked over at Boomeh. She wished she could grab the telephone and call for help, but whom would she call? The Syrian Police were probably the cause of the scene. Ever since Israel became a state twenty-seven years earlier, things had become progressively worse for the Jews living in Syria. Maybe if she spoke to someone outside the country, it would help. *Everyone could be saved – secretly airlifted out of this place,* she thought.

Dried petals and leaves of brown, red, green, violet, and yellow crowded in tall glass jars and aluminum canisters, covering the walls of the small shop. Sophia leaned against a mound of ground cinnamon packed into an open sack, one of many lined up on empty oil cans to create a display. She looked up at the dead animal hanging from its tail over Boomeh's head, beside a jar of dried baby crocodiles, and shuddered. She turned to leave the store.

"Is there anything I can help you with?" the storeowner asked.

"No, thank you," Boomeh answered. Her eyes shifted toward Sophia, who was already walking through the open doorway, and she followed her sister hesitantly outside. A donkey pulling along a cart of watermelons stopped near them. "Fresh fruit!" the vendor yelped beside his cart. Eventually, the small crowds broke up and people around them began moving about, secretly taking with them the panic, the worry, and the pain that had become their inescapable reality after each witnessed injustice.

"A beauty to behold!" The watermelon-seller held up a dissected watermelon and displayed it in the center of the pile. A fragment of the anguished person's cry once again whisked past them. It was the voice of a woman.

"Melon the color of rubies!" the vendor called out once more.

Sophia pivoted from side to side, her ears locked on the desperate pitch of the woman's voice which still floated beyond the conversations in the street.

"Just forget about it," Boomeh said. "Forget you were even here."

She didn't blame her sister Boomeh for not wanting to know what was happening or to whom those screams belonged. It was Boomeh's wedding day.

That night, Sophia's thoughts of the day's events returned as she stood under the wooden beams of the *chupah* at her sister's wedding. She stared at Boomeh, glowing in the moonlight, and she knew that it was important for her older sister to feel safe and happy in her new life. No, she couldn't blame Boomeh for not wanting to know anything about the commotion outside the shop that day. It wouldn't be fair to remind her of the fact that they, together with the rest of the three thousand Jews in Damascus, were prisoners living behind the invisible bars of the Jewish Quarter.

The commotion outside the shop would remind Boomeh of that. She could never escape the fact that the life she was about to begin was that of a Jewish woman whose family never dared to escape Syria, for fear of the tortures of the *Mukhabarat*, or Secret Police. All Jews who held government positions were fired; properties were confiscated, and traveling was restricted. Leaving Syria was forbidden.

Freedom. The word flew above Sophia, its feathers of peace and joy carried away on wings too far to reach. Yet people did leave.

Sophia had dreamt of her own escape. Some Jews attempted to make their way out through Lebanon and Turkey. But only the young and unattached would dare, because the journey was extremely grueling and dangerous. Soon, Boomeh would be attached.

It was possible that the woman's screams that morning had nothing to do with the *Mukhabarat*. Maybe the unknown woman had discovered a dead animal on the road or a lively rodent running into her house. Sophia couldn't blame everything on President Assad and his orders for the *Mukhabarat* to keep his Jews in Damascus chained to the land at all costs. Or could she?

Still, that night she smiled at her sister, who was covered in white lace beneath the *chupah* in their courtyard. Four metal poles held up a blue velvet fabric, suspending it just above their heads. This small canopy made up the *chupah*. Small roses dangled over the front and sides of the velvet cover, their bright colors in sharp contrast to the dark blue hue above their heads.

Boomeh insisted on an orderly ceremony – no children marching and no distractions. The presence of the *Shechinah* was among them, and no one was to take away from the seriousness of the moment. Boomeh bowed her head in prayer next to Jack, her soon-to-be husband, who wore the same fixed smile since the morning, clearly unable to hide his happiness.

Just a few years earlier, Sophia's father had pleaded with her to be nice to her cousin, Jack. She never imagined that he would be her brother-in-law. She remembered that summer when she knotted her skirts at the ankle and darted up the tree with a cluster of carob clenched in her hand. Sophia was always drawn to climbing trees. She positioned herself in between the familiar branches that sustained her weight while she eased herself onto a worn sack covering two crossing branches. This served as a seat. Her green eyes peered through the bushy leaves, choosing the opening which offered her just the right amount of visibility and camouflage. Like a lion, she showed herself only when she was ready. The tree was her domain, set up by her rules, and she could climb that tree as many as one hundred times a day.

She could feel him coming. Any minute he would turn the tight curve in the winding street and open the metal door to her *hohsh*. It was her turn to get back at him for dousing her meal with Allepoan pepper.

Quickly, Sophia reached above her head and pulled another bunch of carob off the tree. Then she watched the open courtyard through the small opening once more as she detached the carob, one by one, off the spotted twig that lay in her skirt. She arranged the curved brown fruit in a neat row displayed in the palm of her left hand, while her right stood by - ready to aim.

Sophia whipped her thick black hair off her face and waited. The sound of footsteps bounced off the high walls of the houses down the street. Her heart raced. She concentrated on the rhythm.

The footsteps halted and the heavy metal door slowly squeaked open enough for her cousin Jack to slip in. He stepped across the stone courtyard, quiet like a mouse, looking up after every few steps. He adjusted his glasses and wiped his sweaty palms on the seat of his pants, heading straight for Sophia's house.

Sophia braced her foot against a sturdy branch. A little closer and he would be walking right into the line of fire! "Go! Go!" she shouted, without even realizing that she was saying the words aloud. She pulled back her arm as far as she could and shot the pieces of carob through the air one by one.

Jack stopped suddenly, squirming in confusion. "What? Where?" He cowered, turning toward the tree while waving his arms in front of him to deter each shot. "Who's there? Stop! Sophia? Stop!" he said, catching a carob and throwing it back at the tree with a hint of laughter as he aimed.

Sophia's mother ran down the stairs of the house, holding on to the black railing for support. Sophia didn't notice her witnessing the entire scene until she was just a few meters away from Jack.

"Sophia Zalta!" her mothered hollered. "Come down from that tree this instant!"

She could never forget the look on her father's face that night. "You are nearly a bat mitzvah," he told her. "What will happen then? Will you still be climbing trees and having running races with the boys, even if they are your cousins?"

"She has her grandmother's fire," Grandpa Yosef said. He would do that from time to time. Sitting quietly in his small wooden chair, he'd give the impression that he wasn't listening, when suddenly he would open his mouth and speak his mind. Then, just as abruptly, he'd return to his silence.

Sophia was thankful for her grandfather's little interruptions, although she could almost always spot the frustration on her father's face after them. Sometimes, she caught her grandfather smirking at the small injustices she would occasionally commit, even after the time she collected a bunch of lizards in her pocket to lure a snake out of the cellar.

After this last incident with her cousin, Sophia told herself that she would change - behave more like her sister - give up her spirit for a couple of approving glances from those around her. It was like sitting in one of those barrels in the cellar with the lid fastened tight. It took the breath right out of her. Her father was right about one thing — she would soon be a bat mitzvah. Maybe she could try to behave. She decided she would.

That was over three years earlier. Now, at fifteen, it seemed like a whispered memory of the past as Sophia pushed up on her toes to see over the *tallit* that was draped across Boomeh and Jack. Besides, none of that mattered, she thought. It didn't even matter that her sister Boomeh would be marrying their curly haired cousin Jack with the sweaty palms and glasses — even though now, he had found a way to flatten his puffy hair down to a minimum and he'd bought nicer glasses.

What did matter was that once Boomeh was married, she would be stuck in Damascus, forever.

In an instant, a "pop" of broken glass penetrated the silence. Shouts of joy reverberated throughout the courtyard. Jack lifted his foot off the shattered glass, signaling the end of the marriage ceremony. Then, he looked up at his bride and smiled.

Ululant cries came from a group of women who threw white *lebas* into the air. Boomeh reached for her mother and then Jack's mother before the strings of the *oud* prompted the guests to pull the bride into a dancing circle. Sophia grabbed hands with the others, their motions lit up by the hanging lightbulbs overhead. The circle of girls picked up speed. Sophia laughed, hoping that this celebration would last throughout Boomeh's life.

Suddenly, a stout woman joined in and held Sophia's hand as she whispered, "*Abalek.*". Sophia had heard that expression before and had always understood it to mean, "Same by you." She turned to the woman whom everyone knew as "The Matchmaker" and said a plain, "Thank you."

Later, when the bride and groom took their seats at the dais, Sophia heard the woman's voice again. "Sit next to me, Rose," she said to Sophia's mother. "Tell me about your other daughter. Three of your guests have already inquired about her for their sons. Where have you been hiding this tall beauty? We must talk."

With her back toward them, Sophia's heart froze.

Rose Zalta patted the matchmaker's hand. "Soon," she answered.

Rose ran her hand down her daughter's curls before moving on to the next guest. Her mother's approval came at a time when she least expected it. Sophia smirked at the thought of their conversation that morning when she had heard the front door slam into its frame. "The photographer is here," her mother had announced.

Sophia jumped up and ran straight into her mother as she walked into the room.

"Sorry ... I'm ... ready."

"Slow down Sophia." Rose Zalta shook her head and combed her hair lightly into place with her fingers.

"I'm ready," Sophia repeated, although the look in her mother's eye told her that she wasn't. Sophia followed her mother's stare traveling down her silk gown and stopping short at her gardening boots. Caked-on mud stuck to their sides, just below her satin hem. "I'll change," Sophia said quickly, without adding that she had put on the boots to anchor a wooden beam into the dirt to secure the wedding *chupah*. It was Gazeem's job. As the caretaker, he was expected to tend to that, but he had been sent to the market to pick up some last-minute things for the celebration that night instead.

At the wedding, her mother slipped into the crowd. Sophia let out a breath, and then searched out her friend Eva, pulling her to the side.

"I was looking for you," Eva said. "Did you meet the matchmaker?"

Sophia rolled her eyes and kicked off her right shoe before stepping onto one of the sofas that framed the courtyard.

"You are a natural, Sophia. It is no wonder the matchmaker has been watching you all night."

"Thanks, Eva."

"What are you doing up there on the sofa?" Eva asked.

Sophia's eyes scanned the crowded courtyard, searching for Eva's cousin. "Where is Linda?" she asked, balancing on one foot.

Eva shook her head. "She's not here … she …"

Sophia jumped off the sofa. "She what?"

"Alright, alright. She left."

A string of questions lined up in Sophia's mind, but all she managed to articulate was, "When?"

"Two days ago, after school."

Sophia knew. "Left" meant "escaped." There were ways to escape, even though no one dared to speak of them — ways planned silently in the heart of every Jew living in Damascus. If you looked closely, you could read it in their eyes - pages and pages of fear and sadness bound together with traces of hope that one day they might successfully break out.

"With whom?" asked Sophia.

"That I can't say." Eva shook her head, uneasiness depicted in her eyes. "I don't even know."

"With the entire family, it would be best," Sophia calculated. "Her grandparents, the grandchildren — all of them. This way," Sophia leaned closer to Eva, "if they all go, there would be no one left behind to face the tortures of the *Mukhabarat*."

"Shhhh!" Eva said.

"Only if you tell me!"

Eva inhaled deeply, the tension in her cheeks increasing as she spoke. "They contacted a man who they thought was trustworthy. He wanted them to meet him outside the Old City because he could not get into the *haret* past the guarded posts."

"Them?"

"Linda and her sister Celia."

"The policemen guard the Jewish Quarter as if it were a prized possession, to protect it from criminals of the worst kind. And who are they?"

"Criminals?" Eva said, finishing her *semboosak*.

"Yes, criminals who have such a tight hold on the Jewish Quarter that we can't even breathe anymore. My father took me to the Synagogue of Jubar on Shabbat. That night, we received a friendly knock at the door from the *Mukhabarat* to make sure we arrived home safely. We can't even travel five kilometers in peace."

"Last night, my brother Eliyahu was playing in the street," said Eva. "It was getting dark when my mother asked me where he was. I opened the door to look outside, and there was Eliyahu – standing next to a man who asked, 'Missing someone?'"

"The *Mukhabarat*?" Sophia asked.

"I think so. The man wasn't Jewish, and who else would know exactly where each one of us lived?"

Sophia sat back in her chair thinking of her brothers and their escape from Syria three years earlier, before the Yom Kippur War, Israel's battle with its neighboring countries. Since then, the house felt empty, and so did she. The worst part was the waiting — waiting for a letter, a phone call or a message, always from some foreign relative in Europe in order to sidetrack the suspicions of the *Mukhabarat*. The letter did come, months later, from a cousin in Italy. Knowing that all mail going to the Jewish Quarter would be censored, the cousin had written that *the family* had been doing some traveling and were relieved to be back *home*.

When Sophia innocently asked her father if they would be leaving as well, he leaned toward her, just inches away from her face. "Do you have any idea how busy our friends in the *Mukhabarat* are? President Assad has made it very clear: Their sole purpose here in the Jewish Quarter is to keep track of every Jew living here. Don't you know that they have spies in our streets, in our businesses, and in *your* school?" That was the last time Sophia had mentioned the subject.

Speeches in honor of the bride and groom began, over the sounds of silverware digging into serving platters filled with steaming lamb, roasted chicken, *ejjeh bakdounez*, tomatoes laced with fresh mint, and *kibbe* eggplant. She listened for her grandfather's voice. His words always seemed to reach her heart and his message was always one of unconditional love.

When her grandfather's speech was over, Sophia turned back to Eva. "When will you know about … her?" she asked, understanding that the mere knowledge of Linda's escape could cost them their lives.

"It could be days, weeks, even years before we find out anything. I don't even think my aunt knows much about it. I mean, she knows what her daughters were planning, but it's hard to tell with these people. There is not much you can find out about them and how safe their routes are."

Sophia pulled a chair from a nearby table, remembering how long it took them to hear from her brothers. She could still hear the screams from that morning's incident outside the shop, but decided to keep it to herself. It probably had nothing to do with her friends anyway.

The men poured their second round of drinks while maids in white uniforms carried stacks of platters and dishes inside. At the end of the table, three women, who were old enough to know almost everything about each guest at the wedding, hovered over a pile of pistachio nutshells as they chewed and observed. Another circle of teenage girls formed itself around Boomeh. Sophia stood, the weight of her pale-green satin gown settling on her hips as she straightened. Her almond-shaped eyes, a shade darker than her gown, narrowed on Boomeh as she sank into her heels. Eva stood beside her. "I hope our friends succeed," Sophia said, without turning.

"So do I," Eva whispered back.

Only later did Sophia find out, that those screams outside the shop belonged to Linda's mother.

2

Rose Zalta walked right past Sophia and dropped the bag of vegetables on the kitchen floor. "Shlomo! Shlomo!" she called.

Sophia sat up on the sofa and watched her mother run in every direction until she noticed her sitting there. "Sophia, where is your father?"

Shlomo Zalta rushed in from his bedroom. "I'm here. What is it?"

Rose motioned to her husband. He followed her into the kitchen. "What is wrong?" Sophia heard her father whispering.

"All morning long, I sat with Yvette. She didn't make a sound. Her face was so pale. She was even too weak to bring a spoon to her mouth." Rose heaved in a breath. "I tried to feed her, but she refused. Finally, she took some broth."

Sophia stood slowly. "Who, Mother?"

"Not now, Sophia," her father answered, his stern tone dismissing her to the front room.

"I would have stayed," Rose continued, "but Yvette's sister brought in some doctor. I never saw him before. He started pulling out herbs and remedies I never heard of. Then he gave her a sedative. Such a kind way about him, that doctor."

"Rose, it will be alright," her husband said softly, leading her to a chair.

"I'm still worried about her. They kidnapped her from her home the day of Boomeh's wedding and left her in a freezer – a butcher's freezer, Shlomo – for two days!"

Sophia popped her head into the kitchen doorway. "Who was left in a freezer?"

Rose Zalta looked away from her daughter.

"I heard you say Yvette. Is that the Yvette who is Linda's mother?" she persisted.

Her parents' silence confirmed her suspicions.

"I was there ... with Boomeh. We heard the screams outside a shop in the Jewish Quarter. It was just down the street from Linda's mother's house. I remember wondering why no one bothered to ask if that woman was alright, or to at least see if she needed help. People I knew were afraid to even look up."

Rose blew her nose into a handkerchief. "They can't look up. Don't you see?"

"I don't want you to start worrying too, Sophia. Your mother is enough," her father said.

"When I heard of Eva's cousins' escape, I was a little

jealous," confessed Sophia. "I thought they were lucky." The scream of the unseen woman outside the flower and herb shop pedaled into her mind. Sophia stared at her father. It was hard to believe that he had taken the blame for her brothers' escape on his own, or was her mother tortured, too?

"Calm down," he told his wife. "Yvette Sasson will be alright."

"How can she be alright? They kidnapped her and stuck her in a meat freezer just because her daughters didn't want to be prisoners in Syria anymore!"

"There is much to tend to right now," Sophia's father continued, looking at his wife. "They found Linda and her sister in a cave, in the mountains northwest of Damascus."

"They found them? How are they?" Sophia asked.

Sophia's father lowered his head.

She pulled on her father's sleeve. "What happened to them? Eva told me secretly that her cousins had left. Are they...?"

Sophia's father didn't need to answer. The pitiful way he looked at his daughter said enough.

Sophia glared at her father and shuddered wildly. "No. No. Linda and Celia? It can't be."

Rose Zalta grabbed her daughter and hugged her. Sophia tried to break away, but her mother held her tightly. "It can't be!" Sophia burst out again.

Her father pushed aside the curtain facing the courtyard. "You mustn't say a word to anyone. Their family doesn't know yet."

"What?" Rose asked. "That Linda and Celia are ... gone?"

"They do know that the *Mukhabarat* has been informed about their daughters' escape. They do not know that they have found them."

Sophia swallowed the lump in her throat. "Then how do you know?"

"Gazeem has a friend at headquarters. He tells him things. All of us will be touched by this. The *Mukhabarat* is still making its agents crazy in search of the safe routes to Beirut. This friend says that they have placed moles all over, hoping to discover them."

"Moles?" Sophia asked.

"Yes, moles – spies meant to penetrate a foreign government or intelligence. Aside from using these moles to penetrate the Israeli Intelligence, the *Mukhabarat* placed sleepers strategically in businesses and neighborhoods. They could be anyone – your friend, your teacher. There is no way of knowing. These sleepers are expected to live as normal people – to disappear into society with the understanding that one day they may be called upon to fulfill a duty."

Sophia squeezed her eyes shut. "I couldn't sleep last night. The shutters banged against the house so hard, I thought that they would break right through the stone walls."

"Honestly, I don't remember ever seeing a storm like that," Rose said. "So much rain."

"Maybe it was Hashem displaying His anger." Sophia choked on her words.

"Aaaayyy." Shlomo Zalta rubbed his temples. "The thunder was deafening."

"Someone has to tell this family what has happened," Rose said.

"The rest of the family has been subject to solitary confinement. When they are released tonight, Murad Sasson's closest friends will be at his house to inform them and to help them make arrangements. I just left the *amid* at headquarters. He assures me that the bodies will be released by tomorrow morning so that burial arrangements can be made. Still, this must be handled delicately to avoid any more violence." Shlomo closed the curtain and withdrew from the window.

Sophia's body went limp with the feeling of hopelessness. This feeling numbed her own passion for a different future. She stepped back from the window, her watery eyes looking up at her mother. "Eva wasn't in school today. Do you think she's alright?"

"Eva's fine," her mother said.

Shlomo watched a few tears stream down his daughter's face. "Take her away, Rose!" he yelled. "She is upset. I don't want her thinking about these things."

Her mother led Sophia to her room. "Try to take a rest, sweetheart. You might feel better."

In her room, Sophia fell onto her bed. Shock was the only thing holding back her tears from streaming down her pale face. But soon they came — tears for Linda and her sister, tears for Linda's mother, tears for Eva and Linda's family, and finally, tears for herself. But those tears came with uncontrollable wailing, for they represented more than the two lives that were taken away from her. With the removal of those lives, came the sentence for her own life – to marry and live in Syria forever.

The Secret Police would be watching, breathing down their necks closer than ever. With the tears she shed, she released her secret dreams of a life of freedom, of a future she thought she was so close to attaining.

Maybe it was never close at all, she reasoned with herself. That may have been part of her tactic. Pretending that she was almost close enough to touch that dream had always kept her going. Kept her hoping. Kept her dreaming. Kept her living.

Now, her unmoving body ached at the pain. All that dreaming had only set her up for the shocking disappointment she could not bear to face. She turned onto her pillow and cried herself to sleep.

3

Although there would be mostly men in attendance, Sophia insisted on going to the funeral the next morning. School closed in protest of the murders. "I'll go with Boomeh," she told her father.

Boomeh continued to spend most of her time and all of her meals with her family, despite the separate apartment she and Jack had moved into beside the staircase. "I'm not ready," Boomeh said, still in her morning robe.

Sophia jumped up. "It's a funeral Boomeh. No one is looking at you."

"Jack is going. I must look presentable."

"Soooo?" Sophia said, trying to draw out a response.

"I'll still need some time."

"Time for what?"

"I need to air out my dress from two days ago."

"So wear the dress you wore yesterday."

"Two days in a row? I don't wear my clothes two days in a row, Sophia!"

Sophia squeezed her eyes tight. "Then I'll go with *you*, Father."

Her father took one look at her puffy eyes. "No," was all he said. She had heard that answer before – flat and defined, with no room for discussion.

It was tradition for Syrian men to protect the women in their lives from any unnecessary unpleasantness, daughters included. The night before was an exception. It was impossible for her father to protect Sophia from the news of her friends. The Jewish Quarter of Damascus measured these escapes. Soon enough, the news would hit her. This event would change things for every Jew living in Damascus. For Sophia, it had changed everything.

Her father forbade her to go to the funeral that day. Sophia crawled back into bed. Her mother did not come to her room, but she did send Huda, the maid, with fried *ejjeh lahmeh* and, later on with some cut-up fruit, in an attempt to get her to eat something. Had her mother brought the food, Sophia would have closed her eyes just to avoid having to talk to anyone. Her mother must have realized this, so she had cleverly sent Huda instead.

"Young Miss," Huda knocked and opened the door, showing her two gold teeth. "Look what we have for you," she said, displaying the food tray.

Sophia pulled her blanket up to her chin and turned over. "No, thank you," she mumbled.

Huda walked to the other side of the bed. "Your mother says that you have not eaten anything today. Your mother says that she is expecting an empty tray."

"Then you eat it."

Huda paused for a moment. "Whatever you wish." She lowered the tray onto the night stand, sliding it beside Sophia's bed. Then she leaned down, smiling artificially so that her gold teeth flashed. Two flies hovered in circles above her veil.

"Thank you," Sophia said, fluffing the covers over her head.

Huda's black-hooded figure disappeared into the hall. Moments later, Sophia heard her voice echoing through the house. "They are here! The masters are here!" Huda announced, waddling down the hall. "I will get the door ... get the door for the masters."

Her father and grandfather walked into the house, their clothing damp and wrinkled.

"We followed the caskets in protest all the way to the American Embassy. But it didn't last long. Soon after, the police positioned fire hoses at close range, shooting water at all of us." Shlomo collapsed onto the sofa. "I heard shots being fired from afar."

Grandpa Yosef plucked off his hat and patted the perspiration on his forehead. "Threatened by the peaceful demonstration, of course," he said sarcastically.

"The more publicity the community can get on this, the better. Assad despises American interference on any level. If the Syrian community in America picks this up and it rises to a political level, our president will be placed on a platform of compromise."

Rose lifted her head from a cabinet she had been

scrubbing. "That may be our only solution." Then she mumbled, "Our president has never cared for anyone but himself. I don't know why he doesn't treat us equally so that we may do well by him and his country."

Grandpa Yosef slipped a *sefer* Mishnah off the shelf and settled into his chair. "Assad is evil, but he is also very shrewd. We must be careful with such a man."

Shlomo sat down beside Grandpa Yosef, chewing on a dried apricot. "Grandpa is right. Everyone thought Assad was lucky to climb the ranks of the Baath Party so quickly, but when he stormed a party meeting, commanding his troops to surround the leaders while he ran as the only presidential candidate in a national election, we all saw what he was capable of doing.

"Now, his impact reaches far wider than Syria. He joined the rest of the Arabs who formed OPEC, and together they have been tightening the noose around the United States of America and any other 'unfriendly states' this year. To be generous, they included the Netherlands, Portugal, Rhodesia, and South Africa.

"OPEC, Egypt, and Syria have instituted further cuts all year long, just to torture the unfriendly countries," Shlomo said, stretching his legs.

Grandpa Yosef cleared his throat. "They have spun world economics into a frenzy, and even though the Arabs have just ended the embargo against the United States, the entire world can still feel its neck in the noose. All this, to punish the West for its support of Israel in the Yom Kippur War."

"Assad is so careful to keep the affliction of his Jews

in Syria out of the world's eye-view, yet he has openly revealed his feelings toward Israel and all who support her," Shlomo said.

"Not many can boast of such a dreadful reign," Grandpa Yosef said with a chuckle.

Shlomo Zalta plucked another dried apricot off the brass tray beside him, its edges fluted with an inlay of turquoise stones. "And don't even think of disagreeing with him. For those who protest his tactics, he has no problem challenging them with arrest, torture, and execution."

Their conversation flitted up to Sophia's bedroom, and she closed her eyes again at the heightened opinions of the political dilemma of the Jews of Syria.

One day seemed to slip into another for Sophia. The once ever-present flicker in her bright green eyes lay dormant against the haze surrounding her irises, the result from days of crying. Some days, she went down to the cellar to work on the *araq*. Mostly she went there to be alone. She fought to find her place in her life again, lately feeling as if someone else was living it. The *araq* she made was hers alone; even her family and friends didn't help with it. They made her feel even more lost, as she was unable to find herself even within the intimate confines of her life.

Linda's house was off-limits the week of the funeral. Though she could already guess her father's response, Sophia approached him anyway to ask if she would be able to pay respects to her friends' family.

Her father answered predictably. "It would only upset you further. The answer is no!" There were times when she might challenge her father, mostly because she found it too difficult to hold herself back, but that week, her body could not even offer a response.

Sometimes she heard their whispers from behind her back; other times, from the adjacent room. Each time they ended unexpectedly the moment they thought that she was listening. She hadn't realized why, until her parents sat her down for a talk weeks later. Before she settled into the sofa beside the ivory-footed end table, she wondered if they knew just how much of her grieving that week was for herself.

They waited for an opportunity to be alone with her. "About the matchmaker," her father said, the night Jack and Boomeh ate at Aunt Rebecca. He pushed a wooden pipe into the waistband of his pants. "I want to know if you are ready."

Sophia pressed her lips together at her father's timing.

Rose Zalta sat beside Sophia, pinching a piece of lint off her sleeve. "Remember, this might be good for you now."

Fragrant vapors of Turkish coffee filled the room. Grandpa Yosef walked in with a cup and saucer and sat in the small backless chair at the edge of the carpet. He tucked his feet beneath the chair and set down his coffee before opening the *sefer* of *mussar*, mouthing the words by heart.

Her mother clapped her hands. "Two boys have asked for you."

"We might as well get started," Shlomo said.

Sophia swept a curl of hair behind her ear and sat

up at the edge of the sofa. "I don't know."

Shlomo Zalta stopped and sat down on the carpet. "There is one nice boy in particular. His name is Benjamin Tawil."

"You mean Benny from the butcher?"

"So you have noticed him before?"

She wanted to say, *His bloody apron always caught my eye,* but instead said, "I don't remember what he looks like."

Rose shifted closer to Sophia. "He is taller since you last saw him, and his teeth are straight now that his braces are off. He is practicing as a *shochet,* although most of the day he studies exclusively."

"The butcher is his father. Benjamin is working for him. But you know, he is the only son, and it is a good, solid business for him lean on." Sophia's father stamped his fist into the palm of his hand. "A good catch, no, Grandpa?"

Grandpa Yosef smiled from his small chair, displaying the state of happiness he was always in. Only those who knew him well enough could detect the trace of sadness that accompanied him as he yearned each day for the coming of the Mashiach and the full and complete presence of the *Shechinah* within their midst.

Sophia gave her grandfather a sideways glance, wondering how much he had to do with all this, and why he hadn't given her some forewarning.

"Benny is Izzy's grandson," Shlomo said, waiting for more recognition from Grandpa Yosef.

"His mother is a Yedid?" Grandfather asked.

"That's the one!"

Grandpa Yosef nodded again.

"You've heard of him, I'm sure. The boy is twenty-one and ready to settle down." Shlomo turned to his daughter. "What do you think?"

She looked up at her father, knowing that this decision could change her life. Although leaving Syria pressed on her thoughts more than ever, the tragedy of the Sasson girls held back the words she wanted to say. Even if she could come up with a better solution to leave the country, even if it was guaranteed to be successful, her success would immediately convert into danger for her family, especially her father and maybe even her mother. She couldn't even think of her grandfather.

Rose stepped in. "Let's give her some room, some time to think."

Sophia stood up quickly. "I'll let you know," she said.

4

The next day, Sophia opened the cellar door and descended the steps with a basket of *katayif*. Marriage was the anchor that would ground her in the place she longed to escape. She felt herself descending deeper and deeper into that place with each step she took down the bumpy stairs cut into the limestone rock of the cellar.

Only *her* footsteps would bring her down her path of life and yet, she could feel herself taking them against her will. But how could she say this to her father? To anyone?

She rinsed out the bottles lined along the wall and poured the fermenting mixture into the copper pot on the stove. Before lighting the flame to boil the *araq*, she fixed a rubber seal where the cover met the top edge of the pot. Her grandfather had always warned her to make sure the pot was sealed before she began. One of his friends had blown up his house from the explosion of *araq* accidentally dripping into the flame below.

In the corner, a vat of even cruder *araq* sat in its early fermenting stages. Sophia twisted it slightly before lifting the lid, swishing the liquid mixture around. She stretched her arm behind the vat and pulled out a broomstick with a flat piece of wood attached to it. Then, she forced it into the mixture and crushed the raisins. The potent vapors of raw *araq* rushed to her head.

Hissing steam hit the top of the pot as the steaming *araq* made its way through the coiled pipe that circled into the sink. Sophia ran the cold water over it, quickly condensing the steam into a liquid that dripped out of the end of the pipe and onto a cotton cloth stretched over a beaten metal pail.

Quickly, she filled up two bottles with a funnel, trying not to breathe in their dizzying vapors, and pushed a cork into each neck before sealing them with the trickling hot wax of a blue candle.

"Just two bottles for my friend Eva. Is that alright?" she had asked Grandpa Yosef before she left the house. "I just want to give her something. I feel really bad."

"It has been your brew from start to finish for a while now. Do with it as you wish," her grandfather told her.

Now, finishing up her work, Sophia suddenly spun around at the sound of shifting between the two fifty-pound bags of rice leaning against the cellar wall. *Probably another worm-snake*, she thought, tilting the overhead light bulb. She looked for the slender snake, which barely had a head or a tail, while walking toward the bags of rice, jabbing one of the sacks with her foot.

Then she heard it again.

Sophia grabbed a rock and threw it against the wall behind the sack. "Come out, snake!" she yelled.

As if following her command, a yellow coin snake slithered over the sack. Its large head led its long body, marked with black spots, until the spots joined together at its tail-like stripes on either side of it.

"I know you," she said, her eyes glued to the snake as she stepped back. "You like to bite, but you're not poisonous." She instinctively tapped her pockets. "Where are those lizards when I need them?"

Sophia picked up the two bottles and placed them underneath the wrapped pastries in her basket. Her stare followed the sliding snake into the dark corner. "I'll just have to chase you out later," she said, running up the stairs.

The dusty and littered walkways of the Jewish Quarter paved her route to her friend Eva's house. Located in the Southeast sector of the old city, *Haret al-Yahud* had shrunk in size. The Christians had chopped into it from the north, and the Muslims from the west and south. Two soldiers at the corner of El Amine and El Hadjara streets guarded the entrance, betraying any assumptions that the government's attention toward the Jewish Quarter had been minimized as well.

Due to the warm weather, the piles of garbage that people tossed out of their windows had decomposed somewhat, which brought an unmistakable stench to the back alleys. The government did clean up the streets once,

Sophia remembered. The country had received word that an important dignitary wished to visit and see how Syria treated its Jews. Immediately, the entire Syrian military had been sent to clean up the Jewish Quarter. Maintaining only the best impression of their so-called "civilized society" was essential to the Syrian government.

Electric wiring draped between the narrow walls of the houses on the street, right above posters of President Hafiz al-Assad, which were framed in patriotic slogans.

Sophia shuddered. Her blood ran cold just at the thought of Assad. Locking them in. Denying them jobs. Amusing himself with their fear, with their hunger, with their torture.

The second floor of a Palestinian home, built with mud and wood, sat awkwardly over its first floor made of stone. She walked quickly to avoid the stares of the two teenaged boys who lived there. In general, Jews moved out of Damascus, but never moved back in. The amount of strange neighbors increased to replace each Jewish family who left Damascus, and although Syrians considered all run-ins with Israel to be a victory, their latest defeat in the 1973 war left the Jews in Syria having to deal with outright volatility from their Palestinian neighbors.

✳   ✳   ✳

The wall to Eva's *hohsh* was hardly visible behind an abandoned house whose roof had caved in from neglect and disrepair. Sophia snatched a rock from the street and rapped on Eva's door. Her eyes sat still on the Jewish star raised in tiny copper pellets on the solid metal door. She fingered the delicate design and wondered if Eva's brother,

Jacob, had fingered it too, that day.

Eva's father insisted on his handicapped son having exactly what he needed, regardless of what other people thought. Identifying practically everything in their home with that bumpy lettering, called Braille, was just one of the ways to accommodate Jacob's blindness. Superstitious people would walk by and gasp at the Braille on the front door and comment at the openness of the way the family handled the boy's condition. Sophia had always attributed such actions to Eva's family's inner strength, and sometimes wondered if the source of the strength was the actions themselves.

Echoes of stone and metal vibrated in the air until Sophia heard the lock unlatch on the other side. It was the caretaker.

"Eva home?"

The caretaker motioned toward the smaller indoor courtyard. An overgrown row of trees led her way to a stone room built off the house, bordered with black and white checkered masonry that was identical to that of the outer courtyard. Eva lay across a bench there, her head hanging over the edge while she fingered the floor design beneath the sandy film. Sophia pressed on the door. It drifted open, creaking its way into the room.

Eva dropped the stone pieces in her hand and turned her head. Her thin, light brown hair swept the floor. "Oh, Sophia! Come in."

"What are you doing?" Sophia asked.

"Nothing much," Eva said. "I found these rocks behind the back wall in the courtyard. I thought they might give off some color for drawing. They are hard as stone. You think they may be good for Jacob? Maybe I could make a game out of it."

"Show me." Sophia knelt down.

Eva threw one in the air and scooped up the rest of them with the same hand just before she caught the one she had thrown. "Maybe even for a jumping game. Or is it silly? What do you think, Sophia?"

"Sounds great," Sophia said tossing one rock left on the floor into the pile.

"Thanks." Eva shrugged.

Sophia set her package on the floor and clasped an arm around Eva's waist. "Hold on," she said and pulled Eva up in one quick motion.

"Ahh! Thanks."

Sophia lifted the basket. "Here," she said, "before I forget. I wanted to bring something … for your family."

"Thanks," Eva said, placing the basket in the corner. "I'll bring them in the house later. I really don't know how you do it, Sophia – a woman, making *araq*." Eva batted her eyelashes. "Then again, nothing about you surprises me anymore."

Sophia nudged her friend. "How are you, Eva?"

Eva dropped her smile and shook her head.

"Maybe we could just talk," Sophia said.

"Whatever you think."

They swung their feet over the stone bench. Eva crossed her legs above a red and gold mosaic pattern on the floor and turned to her friend. "You heard what happened?"

Sophia nodded. "I tried to come. My father wouldn't let."

Eva's eyes dulled her already pale complexion. "I haven't slept."

"It's been a hard week, Eva."

Eva pressed her hands against her cheeks. "Their faces show up whenever I close my eyes. I can't believe that they are gone."

"I have been crying, too," Sophia said. "I'm so sorry, Eva."

"I know how much you wanted this for yourself, Sophia. I'm sorry, too," Eva sobbed.

Sophia eyes filled with tears. She took in a breath and released it along with the tears she hadn't been able to share with anyone that week. They cried together for a while, until Eva said, "There's something else. You know that boy my mother wanted for me? Remember...?" She waited for Sophia to finish off her sentence.

"David – the one who was everything your parents wanted?" Sophia wiped her tears with the edge of her sleeve.

"Yes. The matchmaker called this morning," Eva said softly. "All week, she was asking all kinds of questions about my brother Jacob."

"What kind of questions?" Sophia asked.

"She had all kinds: Why is he blind? Was he born that way? Is anyone else blind? Is it ... contagious?"

"Contagious?" Sophia shrieked. "You are not serious."

"I am. They wanted to know all about him and at the end they decided to forget about the whole thing. My mother says that they are superstitious. I just can't believe it."

"It does sound unbelievable."

Eva dropped her head. "I just don't understand. After everything we've done taking care of Jacob all these years, is it now going to be used against us?"

Sophia grabbed Eva's arm. "Let me tell you something, Eva. Having Jacob is the greatest thing that happened to all of us, and you know it! Everyone knows that blindness is not contagious. If David and his family are too simple to see that, then we don't want them, do we?"

Eva's lips curved into a tight smile. "But David was everything, wasn't he?"

Sophia turned serious, almost feeling guilty about the string of matches her mother had mentioned to her earlier. Then she turned to Eva and her eyes bulged mockingly.

All at once, Eva's laugh blasted through the air. She covered her mouth, muffling her chuckling. Sophia put her arm around her friend, and they laughed until they were practically out of breath. They sat quietly for a while, amidst unspoken thoughts that lingered in the air.

"I understand why Linda and Celia left," Sophia said suddenly.

"Huh?"

"Sometimes I wonder if I belong here at all."

"What do you mean? Where else would you go?" Eva asked.

"It just doesn't seem normal." Sophia pulled the ribbon out of her hair. "My father doesn't even want to send me to school anymore, because I am 'too old to be with boys'. Then what will I do?"

"What are our choices anyway?" Eva asked.

Sophia's head popped up. "We always have choices, Eva. We're just so accustomed to giving up and taking life as it comes. Sometimes we have a responsibility to make things happen!"

"Well, we can't leave, so how much are we going to change?"

"Sometimes I dream. Actually, I dream a lot," Sophia said. "I wish I were in Israel with my brothers, on holy soil, growing and causing others to grow."

"What would you do there all by yourself?"

"I would have my brothers. Maybe I would even open a school for girls – older girls, who want to further their education and someday give over what they have learned. The only higher education here is in science and math and things that make no difference to us now. Even if we were to apply for a teaching position, do you think our headmaster would hire us? Every year, they bring in Muslim teachers to replace the Jewish ones we have. How can we expect Jewish girls to feel a pride in who they are if all we do is educate them in secular goals which they can't even attain?"

"I don't know why you bother dreaming for things you can't have. It's not that I don't want it for you. I just … I just think that sometimes, disappointment is so difficult for me that I'd rather not dream at all."

Sophia looked out the window, where the blue sky draped the *hohsh* wall. "I have to dream, Eva. It is life for me."

The sun shone, rising overhead and warming the cold stones of the courtyard beyond the window of the indoor courtyard where they sat. "It's so quiet out there. Where is everyone?" Sophia asked.

"My parents are paying respects at Linda's house now. It sounds so strange calling it Linda's house. But what else am I supposed to call it?"

"Everything was so sudden." Sophia pulled herself up on a windowsill that was cuddled in a stone niche in the wall.

"I heard that they are really looking for this man." Eva pitched her head to see behind her.

Sophia stopped short. "What man?"

"The one who has the clean routes out of Syria."

"And?"

"And they aren't sure if it is more than one person. I overheard my father and uncle talking. My uncle has a great sense of humor. He asked my father to find out if the routes were for sale."

"But there have always been smugglers."

"Right, smugglers like the ones who made my cousins suffer. But this one is different. They think he is Jewish. They have been looking for him forever. It just came up recently again, you know, after the Yom Kippur War and all."

"Sounds like a real thorn in the side of President Assad."

Eva rubbed her temples. "Sophia, she came to see me before she left."

"Who - Linda?"

Eva nodded. "She looked really nervous. You could tell. She kept looking down at her watch. 'I hope this works,' she said. 'Pray for me,' she repeated over and over again." Eva's last words thinned out as she spoke them.

"And you did pray," Sophia told her.

"Maybe not enough. I'm sick over this. That is why my father forbade me to go to Linda's house. He's worried about me … he knows how close we were."

Sophia jumped off the windowsill and sat down again next to Eva.

Eva turned to her friend, her words cracking in her low tone. "I think … about the summer and our vacations in the mountains." She pressed her back against the bench. "Sophia, remember how she screamed when you pulled a worm right out of the dirt and dangled it in front of her face?"

A painful feeling rose up in Sophia's throat. "Or when she came to visit me when I was sick and dumped my schoolbooks on my bed," she said.

"It's all I think about. I just can't stop."

Sophia rested her head on Eva's shoulder. "Then let's remember," she said. "Maybe it's good to remember."

Then Sophia's mind drifted off again to the safe routes and the legendary man who held them.

5

Sophia pulled open the metal door to her *hohsh* at the sound of someone hammering on it the next morning. An unshaven man appeared in the doorway. "The old man. I need to see him," he said, swaying and rushing past her.

"One moment, please. I will see if my grandfather is up," she said, struggling to reply amiably to this stranger's brazen attitude, although she knew that Grandpa Yosef was up before the birds every morning.

Grandpa Yosef walked to the *hohsh* door himself to greet the man, bringing his guest inside and offering him a pillow in his chair, while Grandpa Yosef sat on a hard and uneven wood-slated chair. Sophia poured water for the two and set the cups before them.

The visitor had his head cupped in his hands. "They told me to come to you. Even my Muslim neighbor suggested it. 'Go to the old man at Zalta's house,' they told me. 'He will know what to do.'"

"I do not have anything special to offer you, but I will try to do my best, with Hashem's help."

The man shifted nervously in his seat. "A Palestinian buyer we have been dealing with has kept the goods we sent him without payment. Every week he tells us that he has the money and is sending it over. After three months, I went over to his store. He admitted that he had no intention of giving us one penny and that he is keeping all the goods. He threatened to make trouble for us if we pursue it any further. Don't you see? I am in real trouble either way. I'm afraid to press this Palestinian further, and I have people to pay, as well. I was counting on that money; this money is the survival of my business! I have a family to support. If I don't come up with either the goods or the money, I am going to have to start begging for food. I really need a miracle here."

"What is this man's name and where is his business?" Grandpa Yosef asked.

The unshaven man opened the tattered paper in his hand. "I have it all written down here. I was going to go to the *Mukhabarat* to see if they could do something about it, but I have a bad feeling about that."

Sophia sprinkled a brass dish with a few handfuls of *bisid* and set it down.

"I have an idea," Grandpa Yosef said. "How much were the goods worth?"

"Hundreds of thousands of liras. Why?"

"Give ten percent of that to charity as soon as you get home."

"That's it? What about my goods?"

"With Hashem's help, they will come."

Sophia wondered how her grandfather could be so sure. Her annoyance for the unshaven man turned to pity as he thanked her grandfather. She stepped outside. Huda held on to the railing, walking up the stairs to the house with the slow swag that usually caused her mother's voice to grow tight with tension. A black cat, waiting by the bottom step, purred as Huda walked by. "I fed you enough yesterday for an entire week, didn't I?" Huda screeched, kicking the cat aside. She climbed the steps, her one-sided conversation subsiding into a quiet mutter as she reached the top slab.

Sophia sneaked past the ornate staircase. She pulled down on the corner fig tree and plucked off a handful of ripe fruit, leaving the tree's branches bouncing in the air. The cat did not hesitate to snatch the figs when Sophia tossed them right up to his paws.

Several meters from the bottom of the staircase, Jack and Boomeh stood by their doorway, peering up at Huda.

"Hi," Sophia said. "What is wrong?"

Jack closed the door to his apartment, smirking. "Oh, it's Mrs. Tawil, the butcher's wife." Sophia almost turned around to see who he was speaking to before she realized that he was teasing her.

"Mrs. Benny Tawil. Does that mean that we don't have to wait on line to buy meat for the holidays anymore?" he asked with an innocent expression on his face. Sophia blushed.

"Jack, be nice," Boomeh said.

"Just having some fun," he said, grinning like a school-boy. Then the grin vanished and he mumbled, "I saw Huda snooping about before. I don't like that Pharaoh around here. She is always with that cat. She smells like cats," he said, his nose twitching. "In my house, my mother did everything. Why do we even need her around?"

"I'm doing our laundry myself, aren't I, Jack?" Boomeh bent over a mound of clothing, turning her dirty laundry inside-out before folding and ironing it all flat. Sophia never asked her sister why she folded her dirty laundry before she washed it; it was as much a part of Boomeh as her homely features. Boomeh carried the basket through the doorway and turned to Sophia. "Huda makes him nervous."

Outside the servants' quarters, where a thin rope stretched twenty feet across the center of a clearing, Boomeh lifted her blouse from the top of the pile and shook out the crisp lines she had just pressed into it before releasing it into a vat of sudsy water. She did this with each article of clothing, each towel, and each sock until the vat was filled and its water had turned gray. Sophia watched Boomeh for a moment before running inside the house and returning outside with some bread with chunks of *labneh* and apricots for the two of them.

The sisters scraped lazily along the *hohsh* wall, chatting and nibbling on the food together. Their features gave no indication whatsoever that they were, in fact, sisters. Sophia always sensed that her father favored Boomeh's soft coloring and light brown hair, so similar to that of her mother's. Boomeh's perfectly groomed appearance was the result of hours spent by a mirror and water basin.

Sophia, on the other hand, stood an entire head taller than her sister. She had strongly defined features and olive skin, framed by thick dark hair that curled only at the edges. She resembled most closely her eldest brother, her father's pride and joy. "But her eyes are her grandmother's, set just like emeralds," Grandpa Yosef would fondly say about her.

Slight gusts of air brushed the sisters' feet, cooling the beads of sweat that formed between the openings in their sandals. In accordance with her orderly ways, Boomeh almost always did exactly what was expected of her, so that sometimes, Sophia found herself hoping that Boomeh would actually do something out of character, shocking her parents long enough to remove what felt like their heavy watch on her every move.

Huda came through the small courtyard off the side of the house, dragging a mound of clean sheets behind her. "*Shlonek*, Sophia!" Huda called out, waving her hand. "Clean sheets today for you!" Sophia waved back, realizing that since Boomeh's wedding, she had gained what seemed like Huda's respect, being the only single woman in the household besides her. Huda started up the stairs, raising the linens up over her head with their corners still brushing the ground.

Sophia's thoughts broke out. "How did you know that Jack was the right one for you, Boomeh?"

Boomeh smiled, adjusting the scarf on her head. "It was the logical thing to do. Besides, I found myself laughing at his jokes, only they weren't at all that funny."

"And?"

"And Father wanted it. Also, it just seemed right. *He* seemed right."

Sophia shivered at the thought, since her impression of Jack had never really changed, even though he did marry her sister. "Is that really enough for you?" she asked with a touch of frustration. A lot of what she said that year was laced with frustration - frustration, irritation, and unspent conviction.

"Precisely," Boomeh said, using the same perfect affirmative which always made Sophia laugh. Boomeh pursed her lips in such a typical Boomeh-like expression that Sophia had no choice but to laugh, and for that moment, marriage didn't seem so frightening and Damascus didn't seem so suffocating.

"You heard about Benny Tawil?" Sophia asked.

"Ma told me about him," Boomeh said. "We all had to do some checking on him."

"It sounds like Father wants me to marry him before our first meeting."

"You know Father. Ever since he was fired by the government…"

"I know." Sophia lowered her voice. "Arabs won't hire Jews and most Jews are forbidden to own businesses. I was surprised that Ma bought me a dress for your wedding altogether."

"So when Father sees a nice family," Boomeh continued, "that's all he wants for us. The fact that Benny is in a family that has a steady business will also be helpful."

"Especially now. But that means that…" Sophia took

in a deep breath, "I'll have to live here."

"Well, where else would you live?" Boomeh asked, as if life existed only within the ancient walls of Damascus.

"Someplace where my goal will mean something, a place where I can use what I have, what Hashem gave me," Sophia said, gazing out at the sky's expanse.

"You think too much, Sophia." Boomeh dismissed her with her hand.

Sophia sat on the edge of the fountain and swirled her hand through the low water, creating a current for the small toad swimming a foot away.

"Don't touch the water!" Boomeh screamed. "There's a lizard!"

"It's a toad, Boomeh. They're harmless. And cute," Sophia said, bending over to see the toad swimming away with its back legs.

Boomeh's nostrils flared. "How can you even sit there?"

Sophia sighed. Benjamin Tawil, the butcher's son. If he were to take over his father's business, that would make him a butcher, too. Somehow, she had never imagined herself married to a butcher. She didn't even like meat.

A single cloud inched overhead and patched the sun with haze here and there. She looked up at that cloud, thinking of her dream of escape and a better future. Her thoughts of marrying in Syria haunted her and, like the cloud, created a constant shadow that darkened the prospect of her bright future.

Boomeh stood over her. "Father pretends not to fully

know about the *araq* you have been making and selling."

Sophia shrugged off Boomeh's stare. "I help Grandpa. Everyone knows that."

Boomeh's head jutted out from between her shoulders. "Girls don't make *araq*, Sophia. They don't climb trees, they don't *accidentally* fall into the river with their clothes on, and they don't make friends with toads either! They sew and cook and help out with the chores. You haven't noticed how forgiving Father has been to you, have you? When was the last time he hollered at you to take off Gazeem's old gardening boots? Or have you finally taken them off for good?"

Sophia looked up, her bright eyes glistening against her dark hair and olive skin. "What are you trying to say, Boomeh?"

"All I'm trying to do is warn you."

"Warn me? About what?"

"I think," Boomeh whispered, "that Father wants you to marry Benny. That is why he is being so nice."

Sophia looked Boomeh straight in the eye. "You think that Father is being so forgiving in order to get on my good side – to get me to trust him about starting a life here – to trust him and marry Benny?!"

"The families will do well together," Boomeh added in her mother's voice. "But you never know how long Father's patience will last. Don't wait too long, little sister."

Sophia gazed at the ripples of water in the cistern, digesting the truth in her sister's words. Then she scooped up an armful of water and thrust it at Boomeh.

"Aaaaah!" Boomeh screamed, looking down at her

soaked blouse. Then she ran, as Sophia knew she would, revenge never working in her favor. Boomeh slowed down and turned around. Sophia dipped her hand into the water, eyeing her sister, just in case Boomeh had thoughts of finishing the conversation.

More shocking than Boomeh's words was the fact that they had come from Boomeh. Sophia always thought that the reason Boomeh was so agreeable to everything was because she didn't know any better. Now, she had actually said something that enlightened Sophia. So that was the reason for her father's tolerance! What bothered Sophia most was that she had been too blind to see it herself.

6
_____

June brought with it fuzzy apricots, citrus fruits of all colors, and the urge to tug at the trunks of date palms to encourage a succession of falling sticky clusters. Blooming orange trees pitched against the inside corners of the *hohsh* walls dotted with ladybugs. The scents of Arabic jasmine and roses swayed in the air.

Rose Zalta took a job as a midwife, keeping a canvas bag always filled with sterile linens and supplies. The unshaven man did get paid for his goods as soon as Grandpa Yosef approached their Palestinian neighbor about it. The man told Grandpa Yosef that he had listened to his advice and had given the *ma'aser* from the goods. Sure enough, the money he was owed came through! He thanked Grandpa Yosef over and over again. Grandpa Yosef thanked Hashem.

No one spoke of the Sassons or of their attempted

escape. Sophia lived almost against her will, as her dreams of living in Eretz Yisrael were halted, and even worse, never dared uttered to her father. People yearned for simplicity and prayed for the uneventful. Life in the Jewish Quarter seemed to just go around in circles, never leaving the high stone walls.

Somehow, June also brought with it a feeling of newness and starting over — a feeling which prompted Sophia's decision to go out for the first time. Aside from pleasing her parents, she wanted to begin something eventful.

Inside her bedroom, Sophia bent over a water basin, barely ready. Someone had thrown a hand grenade over a *hohsh* wall down the street, and Sophia, along with the rest of the neighborhood, had been bound to the house because of the incident. The hot water tank sat empty all day because no one was allowed to go out to the well to refill it. The courtyard was declared dangerous until they caught the man who threw the hand grenade. With no alternative, Sophia was forced to wash up with a small puddle of water in a shallow basin.

She heard a voice coming from the front hall. *He's already here?* She panicked. Twisting her fingertips, she spiraled her hair into a knot. *Where is Mother?* Her stomach turned over as she opened the door a crack to take a peek at the butcher's son.

She sagged with relief at the sight of their caretaker. *Thank goodness! It's only Gazeem.* She closed the door and welcomed his mumbling voice, for it kept her nervousness from peaking while she finished dressing. The thought of leaving Syria never left her mind, only now it was sandwiched between her nerves for the day.

A knock at the bedroom door made her whirl around. "Ma!" Sophia hugged her mother. "Thank G-d you made it. Are you alright?"

"*You* were worried? I'm fine, thank you. You heard about the grenade?"

"I wasn't sure you would make it, Ma. Boomeh told me that you were helping out with a baby today and I didn't want you to risk anything by trying to get back."

"I left early this morning, and someone took over for me. I hurried over as soon as I heard it was safe to come home. I wanted to be here for you."

"Let's hope it stays safe out there." Sophia patted her light blue skirt, banded wide around the waist where her white cotton blouse tucked into it firmly.

"Very pretty," Rose said, nodding with approval. She removed a turquoise pin from her own lapel. "Take this. I think it will look nice with that blouse. Be careful. It's very sharp." She pulled a loose hair off Sophia's shoulder.

"Is Huda out there?"

"Why, do you need her?"

"Ma, Huda is so strange. Yesterday, I asked her where my dress was. She remembered washing it but she doesn't remember where she put it. She told me that in Saudi Arabia, she had two maids to take care of her. One to cook, and the other to clean and do the laundry. She is always talking about her husband, Rashid. Is she really a princess?" Sophia bent her head, twisting her hair into a bun.

"The royal family in Saudi Arabia is so huge; practically everyone living there is either royalty or serving royalty. Huda was supposedly the fourth wife of a Saudi prince. One day, he stood up, repeated the words 'I divorce you' three times, and that was it for Huda. She left with her dowry, but had nowhere to go. That was twenty years ago. The man your father does business with employed her for some time in Saudi Arabia. This is her first time out of the country, and we hired her. That is all we know about her," Rose Zalta said.

"If she came from such royalty, why is she always rubbing insects between her fingers and kicking cats across the courtyard?" Sophia asked, looking up at her mother.

"I wonder sometimes about Huda." Her mother shook her head, inching open the bedroom door. Then she took Sophia's hands in hers. "If this is your *naseeb*, let's pray to G-d that you see it."

Sophia kissed her mother's hand. "Thank you, Mother."

"I'm going to put out some fruit," Rose said. Leaving the bedroom door open a crack, she hurried down the hall.

Gazeem came through the front door for the second time, holding a sack of pistachio nuts in his arms. "I bought this variety in Aleppo," he said, tossing the sack onto the floor. "Much more delicious than those from Iran, no matter what those Persians tell you."

"Thank you, Gazeem," Sophia heard her father say before slamming the front door shut. "What did you find out about the disturbances earlier?"

"It was nothing. Just a drunk Palestinian who couldn't control his tongue – mouthing off to anyone who would listen about 'Israel and its dirty Jews'. I wish they would just keep their opinions to themselves. They give the rest of us Arabs a bad name." Gazeem reset the grubby turban on his head.

Huda shuffled by, her sandy slippers barely lifting off the floor. Huda refused to wear anything that would mask her natural beauty, so that she always smelled like a Bedouin on a hot summer day. And today, with all his work in the courtyard, Gazeem looked the way Huda smelled.

Shlomo smacked a pillow with the inside of his palm and placed it in the corner of the sofa in the front room. "Still," he said to Gazeem, "we can't be too careful. With each additional year, the Palestinian presence has increased steadily. I'm not even referring to the rest of Syria. I'm talking about right here in the Jewish Quarter."

Huda stepped out of the shadows, speaking to no one in particular. "When I was a girl, women went out of their houses only three times in their lives – to the home of their bridegrooms, to the funeral of their parents, and to their own graves." Then she stretched her foot over the edge of the Persian carpet, brushing the silk fringes with her bare toes.

"Thank you, Huda," Sophia's mother said, leading Huda to the door. "That is all for tonight."

Grandpa Yosef looked up from his chair and smiled as Sophia walked into the room. Gazeem and Huda had slipped out of sight.

And then Benny came.

Sophia took in a deep breath. "Hashem, if this is the right thing, at the right time, in the right country, please let me see it," she mumbled under her breath before stepping forward. All her preconceived hopes and aspirations of whom she would marry and what kind of life she would live suddenly shrunk, cowering behind Benny and his wide smile. Could he be all those things for her?

Benny laughed easily with Sophia's father, seemingly unbound by the usual insecurities of a first meeting. He did manage to give Sophia a few seconds of recognition when he thanked her for saying 'yes' to the matchmaker.

Sophia knew that her father would want a few minutes alone with Benny before she entered the room. "I forgot my hat," she said, excusing herself for a few minutes.

At last, Sophia and Benny left the house together. Benny had insisted on taking her out in the daytime, and Sophia couldn't figure out why, until, as they were walking, Benny pointed out his father's butcher shop and casually suggested that they stop in. Sophia let out a deep breath. She hoped that if he was the right one for her, life would mean more than having a generous supply of meat and chicken.

She tried to smile as she looked up at the display of opened carcasses hanging from bloody hooks against the wall. A woman waiting at the scale observed the scene and smirked, realizing that Sophia was not there to buy anything. "This is my son," Benny's father said to a customer, gesturing at Benny while wiping his knife back and forth against his stained apron. Then he winked at his son and smiled broadly.

Sophia shrank back, her cheeks reddening.

When they stepped back onto the street, the afternoon heat had risen, so that practically everything was hot to the touch. The Lebanese Mountains halted the wet winds that brushed in from the Mediterranean Sea, preventing them from reaching Damascus, just eighty kilometers away. Sophia wiped her moist brow, dreading the continuous water cycle that kept rainfall in the Syrian capital down to a few inches a year.

Benny turned to her. "How about a cold drink?"

"That would be great," Sophia replied.

They walked around winding lanes and through an ancient Roman arch, which capped Azaryet Street. So sure and confident was the Roman Empire, building arches, colonnades and theaters as if the world would always live by their standard. Their window in time had passed so that now, the best they could do was just look on at the world through the crumpled, decaying stones of their barbaric empire. Assad had certainly left his mark in Syria. Would he crumble just as the many empires before him?

She wondered why the matchmaker had not reminded her to wear flat shoes. As it was, Benny's stout figure barely reached her forehead.

A small crowd stood outside an open café. Benny hurried inside the café past the crowd. Sophia followed. "Now we can pick what table we want," he whispered to her.

The owner stood and pulled out two straw stools at a small table. Sophia waited for Benny to sit. Benny turned around. "I think that table would be better," he said. The next table closer to the entrance didn't seem to make Benny any happier. A beam of sunlight shone into the café, aimed directly at his left eye. "Maybe this one would be better," he said pointing to a different seat.

Sophia nodded and they switched to a table whose legs stood unsteadily on a dusty crimson rag. She eased herself slowly onto the hard wicker stool, waiting for Benny to change his mind again. A picture of Assad hung on the green wall of peeling paint over Benny's head, and she found herself unconsciously turning away from it.

A turbaned waiter, not much older than twelve years old, placed an *argilah* in the center of their table and offered to set a chunk of burning coals over the tobacco at the top of the *argilah*. She was grateful when Benny declined and instead ordered salted olives and carrot juice.

Sophia fiddled with her mother's pin that she had decided to wear in her bun instead of on her blouse, as her mother had suggested. She was unable to find the rubber tip needed to fasten the pin through her buttonhole. Instead, the pin found its place fastening the knot of thick curls pulled back neatly at the back of her head.

Black flies buzzed over a casserole of baklava, dipping their tentacles into the sugary syrup that dripped down the sides. "How old are you?" Benny asked. Olive juice soaked his chin.

"Sixteen," she answered, hating to say her age which labeled her eligible for marriage. "Do you work with your father?"

"Yes, for a part of the day. Since I became a *shochet*, I am more involved with the business. It can easily turn into a full-time job. Nice, yes?"

Sophia thought about the bloody carcasses hanging from their hooks leaning against white walls streaked with blood. Before she could stop herself, she said, "You do have an eye-catching display at the shop."

His face lightened up and he gave a surprised snort. "I leave that up to my father. I am trying to concentrate on the slaughtering. Mostly I take care of the gutting."

Gutting? Sophia reached for her glass and took a sip of carrot juice. The smooth liquid cooled her instantly.

"Chickens." He nodded. "I mostly gut chickens. Turkeys are the real challenge for me. Their insides are like thick elastic."

"Really?" Sophia said, revolted by the thought. She picked up a shriveled olive from the metal saucer. The picture of the boy in front of her sharpened while her notions of marrying a scholar slowly faded.

"Yesterday, I wrestled with a turkey, bloodying my entire arm to gut the thing. My hands were trembling and before I knew it, that bird sprang out of my hands and hit the opposite wall." Benny pushed back his stool, as if acting out the scene. "I fell onto the table, just missing the sharp saw." His contagious laugh filled the small shop.

"It sounds like you enjoy what you do," Sophia said, choosing her words.

"I love it!" Benny said.

Suddenly, Sophia watched Benny's smile drop from his face. She didn't understand why, until she followed his eyes, which were tracing the steps of a small red scorpion as it made its way across the adjacent table. Benny had a frightened look on his face and he turned to her, pale. Without thinking, Sophia pulled out the pin sticking up from her hair and stabbed the scorpion, while holding down its poisonous tail with the metal saucer from the table.

Sophia's heart raced and she could see the look of surprise in Benny's eyes. The waiter, who assumed that it was Benny who had taken care of the job, thanked him and tossed the lifeless scorpion into the trash before wiping her mother's pin dry. Benny jumped up and stepped onto the street. His head jerked forward as if he was about to vomit.

Regret stabbed Sophia's thoughts and she shrank back into her seat. "Thank you," she said to the waiter as he returned the pin to her. She held it by a turquoise stone edged in silver and slid it into her pocket. For a moment, she thought about rinsing it off and putting it back into her hair, but something told her not to.

Benny stepped in, tossed a few coins onto the table, and motioned to Sophia to join him outside. She didn't mention anything to Benny about the scorpion; on the contrary, he seemed to be in complete control now, and she thought talking about it might embarrass him. "*Imshe yulla*! Move on already!" he screamed out at the donkeys and goats that blocked their path. Arab children ran in the street, playing barefoot beside a steady stream that leaked from a ruptured pipe. Benny picked up a small stone and skipped it across the water. The children ran up to him in a frenzy, circling him with their outstretched palms, hoping for a donation. Benny merrily slapped each one of their palms. The children squealed and screamed out to their mothers nearby.

"I like children. Do you?" he asked.

"Uh huh." Sophia nodded stiffly, watching one of the boys lick the inside of his burning palm and blow on it softly.

An old man poured some water from a goatskin pouch hanging across his shoulder into a rusty metal cup, which he then shoved before them. Benny waved him off curtly. "There must be a better way to serve water these days," he said.

They walked along a stony road toward Sophia's *hohsh*. Benny spoke more about his plans for expanding the family business. "I try to talk to my father, tell him about making changes and taking chances. My mother says I have a knack for it. I figure, if my father can run the store, I can start spreading out like I have always wanted my father to do."

He was still going strong even after she opened the door to her *hohsh*. "There is room for another butcher in Damascus. It's just those Arabs. They won't give us the business."

Sophia thought about the mortified look that Benny had when she had killed the scorpion and wondered how he would even work in the family business, never mind expand it.

Grandpa Yosef was resting against the wall of the staircase, so quiet and still that Benny did not even notice him and just continued talking.

Sophia listened to Benny as he mapped out his life before her, almost feeling jealous at how certain he was about his future. For the first time, her dreams of leaving Syria seemed small in her eyes as she questioned their connection to reality.

"There are so many possibilities, and I am ready for them all. Of course," he said, turning to Sophia, "they tell me it is important to start a family first. After I get that out of the way, I can concentrate on the business. Would that be a possibility for you?"

Sophia stood shocked and unprepared. Even though she did not answer his question, she had already made up her mind.

7

"So?" her father asked her before dinner.

"So, what?" Sophia answered, tightening the door hinge on the cabinet in the front room with a screwdriver.

Her father slipped the screwdriver out of her hand. "Benny. What did you think about him?"

Sophia hid her smile from her father. "I don't know."

"Well, either you like him or you don't. What don't you know?"

"Shlomo, it isn't always that simple," Rose said, sitting down on the sofa, prepared for a real talk. "Did you have a nice time?"

"He is nice. I guess he tried to make me feel comfortable even though I was a little nervous."

"That's normal," her mother said, brushing out a wrinkle in the sofa cushion. "Where did you go?"

"We went for a walk and then we stopped for a drink at the café." Sophia paused, trying to pull her thoughts around the scorpion story. "And then we walked some more before he brought me home. I don't think he is serious about learning. It sounded like he went through his studies just so that he could become a *shochet* and further himself in the family business."

"Is that a problem?" her father asked.

Sophia shrugged her shoulders. "It's just that I thought he was a scholar."

Rose inched closer. "Did you enjoy his company?"

Her father huffed and began to pace.

"He likes to talk a lot – about himself. And he switched his seat three times."

"Enough!" her father roared. "Do you want to go out again with him, or not?"

Sophia's body stiffened. "No."

At the confidence of her definitive response, her father finally looked up. He stood quiet for a minute and then sat down next to his wife.

"Can you at least tell us why, so that we will have something to tell the matchmaker?" Rose pleaded.

"What's wrong with … 'she's not interested' or 'he is very nice, but not her type'?" Sophia said. "Tell her whatever you want."

"Sophia?" her father questioned in a disciplining tone.

"I don't know … he's a butcher. He is not really my type. He is shorter than me. He makes me a little nervous. Why don't you ask the matchmaker? Maybe he doesn't want to see me again. Maybe *he* doesn't think that *I* am *his* type, either."

Her father slapped his legs with the palms of his hands. "That's it, Rose. Contact the matchmaker! Contact her and find out."

That night, the matchmaker beat Rose to the question. She came running through the courtyard to tell them the news personally.

Norma, the matchmaker did not even ease herself into the conversation. "Benny is wild over your daughter. What a blessing!"

"That's nice," Rose said, looking over her shoulder to see her husband's reaction.

Sophia was in the kitchen, where she could hear everything without being seen. She dropped a handful of string beans onto the counter and began snapping off the edges and tossing the beans into a bowl.

"He does not even want to wait. He is convinced that she is the woman for him. His mother told him to slow down, but he is insistent on knowing immediately what her plans are. So tell me: Do we have a match?"

"Maybe," her father said.

Sophia twisted a bean between her fingertips, peering at the white wall in front of her.

Rose stared at her husband. "Norma, this is nice news and we would like to discuss it with Sophia. I will let you know soon."

"I wouldn't wait too long. You cannot imagine how a good boy is hard to come by. Don't forget, he has a family business to go into – a nice stable income for your daughter." The woman elbowed Rose. "Ah, what every mother wants for her daughter, given of course, that the boy qualifies." She picked up her canvas bag. "I'll be by tomorrow. You should know by then. Even if the girl has her doubts, there is nothing like a second meeting to make up one's mind. I know Benny won't protest." With that, she turned and left, waddling down the steps, her canvas bag swinging alongside her.

"What now?" Rose asked, watching from the window in the front room as the matchmaker made her way across the courtyard.

"I know that you are listening, young lady," Sophia's father said loudly, "so you might as well come out now."

Sophia shrugged her shoulders. "I didn't think that … that he was even interested."

"Do you think you might want to see him again? Give it another try?" her father asked.

"I thought we had finished that discussion," Sophia said.

"Just once more," her mother begged. "And after that, if you really don't want to go, you don't have to."

Sophia looked intently at her mother and remembered hearing that before. When she was six and didn't want to eat her chicken liver, it had been, *just one more taste, and then if you really don't want to finish the rest, you don't have to.* It hadn't made a difference then. Why should it now? She had always been confident in her decisions. Why were they making her doubt herself?

She felt trapped – like there was no way out but through the fire. "Alright," she said finally. "Once more –

but that's it! Whatever I decide about him after that is my decision."

Her father nodded silently, looking on at her mother, who was smiling.

After a dinner of *bizeh b'jurah*, Sophia opened the door to the cellar to agitate a new batch of *araq*. One of the lights had gone out, but she didn't mind the dimness. It helped her to focus on what she was doing, while blurring the unnecessary details. She wished that her life could follow a consistent trail so that she could keep focused on the important things, if she could even figure out what those things were. She smashed the raisins with the wooden paddle, angry that she had to go through a second meeting. She knew that she had made the right decision about Benny, but couldn't help but feel sorry for her parents, knowing the disappointment they were feeling. Boomeh married the first boy she went out with – the first person whom her father chose. Boomeh knew right away. But so did Sophia.

Her instincts were irrelevant now, because a deal was a deal. She had given them her word. A word that she hoped wouldn't speak for her, weaken her, or trap her!

What was the worst that could happen? She tried to reason with herself. She would have another glass of carrot juice and make sure to stay away from any scorpions. What had Benny liked about the date, anyway? The scorpion incident was the only thing that had really "happened." Maybe that was his favorite part? If so, he had a strange sense of humor. She would have to keep an eye on him, she decided. Perhaps their next meeting should be a little more private, with fewer distractions. She might even be able to get to know the real Benny. She would give it a chance, like she had promised. She made a mental note to have her mother mention the privacy aspect to the matchmaker.

Then, her thoughts turned, and her anger began to rise. She had no one but herself to blame for starting this big mess. If she had just kept loyal to her dream, none of this would have happened. If she had stayed stubborn, refusing to meet anyone or do anything, then her parents probably would have *gladly* thrown her out of the house, and who knows how close she could have been to leaving Syria…

She didn't realize what a good job she had done at crushing the fruity mixture until she felt the alcohol stinging her nose just from having agitated the brew. When she banged down on the lid to fasten it, the wooden paddle fell to the floor against the wall, adjacent to the sink. She reached down along the dusty floor to pick it up, hoping she wouldn't find anything moving there.

Ah, there was the paddle. It had wedged itself into the corner. Sophia tried to slip her fingers underneath to lift it, but it wouldn't give. Peering closely, she noticed that a piece of cardboard was fixing it in its place. She wrapped her arms around the vat and shifted it from side to side, until she had freed the paddle from the piece of cardboard. She stood the paddle upright and dusted off the cardboard, studying its torn edges. It looked like the side of a corrugated brown box. When she flipped it over, she saw, by the glow of the single light bulb in the room, an unmistakable drawing. Even in the dim light, the red ink seemed to stand above its surface, etched out in the darkness.

Her eyes darted along the intersecting red lines, trying to make sense of it. The lines all met at horizontally parallel points and then branched out. Stick-figure illustrations of men and single letters in Arabic sporadically dotted the drawing. A broken line ran down the right edge with the picture of a boat on it.

She remembered the stories Grandpa Yosef spoke of and wondered if this was just an illustration of his favorite one. She leaned over the side of the vat and tucked the cardboard behind it, just in case her grandfather had thoughts of visiting it again.

Then she began putting her equipment away and washing up, all the while wondering if she would be able to share sweet memories with her own grandchildren one day – memories that would make her and them feel warm all over, like the ones her grandfather shared with her.

The next time she stepped through the courtyard, it was with Benny. After asking for their second meeting to be a little more private, lunch at his house, together with his parents, was not what she had expected.

8

"He is just not for me," she told her mother when she returned.

"Because you wanted a more private meeting?" her father asked, raising his voice.

"No ... well, yes ... but that's not the reason." The words she wanted to say tangled together in a heap and left her.

"You would have to meet his parents sooner or later," Rose said.

"His parents were not the problem."

"Even though we agreed to let this be your decision, I just want you to know that at the same time, you are giving up a big opportunity," her mother said.

"I know," Sophia said, glancing at her father, who had not looked at her since she walked in. He continued to busy himself quietly around them, like he usually did when he was thinking of the right words to say. *So different from the butcher's son*, thought Sophia.

"We gave her the choice," her father said finally. "If it's not him, it will be someone else."

"Thank you, Father." Sophia jumped up and kissed her father's hand twice. He sighed at her freedom of choice.

Later, she wiped the layer of oil off her lips with her fingers after biting into a pancake of *ejjeh lahmeh*. Her father raised his eyebrows until she could see the wrinkles in his forehead and then handed her a napkin. Even with his humorous gesture, the feeling of disappointment seemed to hover over them all.

She alone sensed her feelings of guilt. Grandpa Yosef brought his plate to the sink. He opened the door, holding his last piece of bread in his hand.

"Grandp-" Sophia started after him, but he didn't hear. She pushed the screen door open and followed him outside to the open room in the courtyard where they used to hold prayers. Grandpa Yosef picked small pieces from the leftover slice of bread in his hand and lined them up on a ledge outside the room, each one apart from the next, shaping them into just the right size "for the mother bird to carry to her young," as he'd once explained to Sophia when she was little.

Grandpa sat in his usual spot at the bottom of the staircase. Sophia stood beside him, waiting for her grandfather's wise words. The tree leaves turned dark green, their trunks black, and the walls of the *hohsh* turned dark gray. Shadows hovered in the cistern as the sky darkened and night began to fall.

"Maybe I should be more obedient and dependable like Boomeh. Maybe everything would just be easier that way," Sophia mumbled under her breath.

Grandpa Yosef looked straight ahead. "Your Grandmother Sophia always knew what she wanted."

Sophia watched her grandfather's deep blue eyes darkening with the disappearance of day. "Trust your perception of clarity, Sophia, because it can leave you as quickly as a flash of lightening in the night wilderness – and once that flash is gone, you may be forced to find your way in darkness and confusion."

"Grandpa," Sophia said, "I knew from the first meeting that he was not for me. They made me — I mean … asked me to go out a second time just to be sure." She blew at the wisps of hair that fell over her eye. "Benny talks a lot, and yet he doesn't have the confidence I imagined in a husband. Do you know what I mean?"

"One coin in a jar can make a great deal of noise," Grandpa Yosef said.

"He is not what I want," Sophia said.

"Just be certain that he is not what you need."

"What I need? I need someone kind. Benny was kind … some of the time."

"And?" Grandpa Yosef asked.

"And I need someone responsible, someone I can rely on. Benny kept looking for a better table, a better solution to water in a goatskin pouch, a better business plan." She threw her hands up. "I know I am not perfect. That is exactly why I need someone sensible. I don't want to have to be at the mercy of his latest scheme."

"There is nothing like the annulment of doubts, which this second meeting has provided for you. Fortunately, you know what you need and have already recognized his attributes, which he has so anxiously revealed. In this way, it has been quick and easy for you. *Chalas!*" He flicked the back of his hand in the air as if dismissing Benny himself. "Consider yourself lucky."

"What about Father and Mother?" She pointed toward the house. "They look so depressed in there. I do understand. And I know," Sophia lowered her voice to a whisper, "that Father is out of a job now. Aside from the wedding, there are living costs to stay married that I am sure he is concerned about."

An expression of sadness crept across her face. "In their eyes," Sophia said, "Benny was the best catch around, with a business that would take care of me. I haven't seen them smile once since I told them that I was not interested in him anymore."

Grandpa Yosef caught her gaze, lifting her eyes to meet his. "Hashem will send you the right one at the right time, no matter where you may be. And when that happens, we will all have reason to celebrate."

She sat up. "But how will I know when it's the right one?" she asked him.

"Hashem has a way of laying out one's path," Grandpa said. "All you have to do is stand back and watch patiently."

Then he quoted from *Sefer Mishlei*, "'Better a piece of dry bread and tranquility with it, than a house full of feasting with strife.'"

Sophia snuggled against her grandfather's words, while they cut smoothly through her worries. And with the absence of worry, her thoughts began to accommodate the prospect of new risks, regardless of their dangers.

9

It was as if Eva had picked up on Sophia's daring thoughts the next day.

"What's the matter?" Sophia asked, opening the door for Eva and immediately noticing the concerned look on her friend's face.

Eva fanned herself. "One of the guards stopped an Arab before at the gates as he was trying to enter the *haret*. And there he was, that same guard, outside your *hohsh* just now. I'm telling you, they seem to literally follow us around!"

It was as if the guard was coming to imprison her for her thoughts. "Probably doing his rounds, still looking for that man who mapped out the safe routes."

"You don't forget a thing, Sophia Zalta, do you?" Eva handed a plate of pastries to Sophia. "Try one."

Sophia munched on a baklava. "This is delicious.

What is the occasion?"

"My grandmother made them. Rememeber David, the boy my parents really wanted for me?"

"The one who was everything?"

"Yes, him. We met two days ago. My grandmother baked these to honor the occasion."

"What about Jacob?" Sophia asked dramatically. "You didn't have to get rid of him, did you?"

Eva laughed. "No. They sort of apologized to the *dallal* for that. But it doesn't matter anyway. It didn't work out. He wasn't for me."

"Did you realize sooner because of Jacob, because of the way they reacted to his special needs?"

Eva's eyes were watery. "I guess I did."

"I think you are lucky," Sophia said.

"Because of Jacob?"

Sophia nodded.

"I never used to think that way," Eva said. "Jacob was always my responsibility. Everything in my home had to work for him – the special Braille writing, the special teachers, the special foods for his allergies. Sometimes I'd get annoyed with it all, and then I'd feel guilty about it. But now I am starting to see things differently. I enjoy Jacob. I really do. Everything is truer and more meaningful with him around. You helped me see that, Sophia."

As she spoke, Eva wove Sophia's hair into a braid and fastened it with a rolled-up leaf from a fig tree. "There," she said. "Now that looks better than your usual bun, doesn't it?"

Sophia looked into a small section of mosaic that

was made of tiny mirrored squares set in a pattern on the wall. "I have no patience to do my hair, Eva."

"Well, there is nothing else to do around here. "

"There is always school."

"I'm not like you, Sophia. I can't get decent grades."

"And what would decent grades do for you?"

"For starters, it would make my father happy."

Sophia laughed.

"Well, why do *you* study, Sophia?"

"Jewish women in Syria cannot hold a government position, Eva, remember? They can't hold a professional one, either. Neither can the men. It is hard enough for a Jewish male to get a job at all. I can't imagine anyone hiring a female."

"So?"

"I guess I study for myself then."

"For yourself?"

"Why should we impose their standards on ourselves? They think that they are doing us a favor by giving us an education that we can't use. This way, when the dignitaries come in, they can show them how nicely they treat their Jews. Just because Assad wants to forbid us from growing, doesn't mean that we have to comply. While we are here, we should want to be the best that we can be, regardless of their tactics."

"What if my best will never come from school?" Eva asked.

"Then you had better find out where it will come from."

"Sometimes I feel like school is just our holding pen

until we discover our husbands."

"I know how you feel," Sophia said. "I have been going out, too."

"Really?"

Sophia stood up, shaking a loose stone out of her sandal. "It didn't work out, either."

Eva slumped onto a bench. "So what are we going to do?"

"I am out of ideas."

"Me too," said Eva.

Sophia sat up. "There is something I have for you." She rummaged through her pocket and pulled out a hand-kerchief tied in a knot. When she unraveled it, small pieces of coal rolled against each other in the folds of the cotton.

"What is that?" Eva asked.

"I know how good you are at drawing. If you press lightly enough on these coals," Sophia said, demonstrating on the stone windowsill with the tip of a coal, "you can be somewhat precise."

"Where did you find these?" Eva asked.

"They're mountain coals," Sophia said. She rubbed her hands roughly against her skirt, soiling it instantly. "Boomeh's husband used them to mark up and measure while he was fixing their apartment. He bought an entire box because it was such a good deal. When their home began looking like the inside of a coal mine, Boomeh made him get rid of them."

Eva leaned over, laughing.

Sophia handed her one of the black sticks.

"You have a whole box of these?"

"Under my bed. Boomeh begged me to hide them from Jack."

"Maybe I will have a try." Eva took the coal in her hand and drew a small bird, using the thin line Sophia had drawn as the back and tail.

"Wow," Sophia said. "You are really good."

"You think so?"

"Every time you finish a drawing, grade yourself. I'm sure you will find that you have very good grades indeed."

Eva looked up, her frizzy hair covering most of her freckled cheeks. "Thanks, Sophia."

Sophia walked her friend to the door and waved good-bye. Then she snuck a quick glance up and down the street, wondering if she would discover the guard or the man with the safe routes they were all searching for.

10

When Sophia set up a new trap for the snake in the cellar; when summer fruit began to turn its ripest; when her mother stopped scrubbing the cabinet doors until her skin split, and when the idea of leaving Syria sharpened in her mind, Sophia continued making and delivering bottles of *araq*. Today, as she set out to deliver her latest bottles, she reviewed her list of deliveries and began forming a delivery route in her head.

Carefully, she scooped up a half dozen bottles and set them in the cart at the top of the steps outside the cellar. She looked around to avoid Jack and the sly look he gave her every time he thought he was capable of incriminating her. The courtyard was empty. She came down for more, leaving the bulk of it behind for Grandpa Yosef to deliver to the *souk* that week.

Sophia found herself filling almost seven dozen bottles a week. There was a continuing waiting list of buyers since Haj Ibrahim, one of the tanners at the *souk*, insisted that the *araq* with the Star of David painted over it brought him twin sons after his eleven girls. "Golden *Araq*" and "Heavenly *Araq*" were some of the names people began calling Sophia's popular *araq*. Some suggested that her grandfather take the Star of David off his *araq*, because so many from all over were drinking it, but Grandpa Yosef said that maybe it was the Star of David which had made the *araq* famous and not the other way around.

The quick goodbye she gave to her mother prevented any more discussions about Benny. Even worse than the drawn-out discussions was the small talk everyone made to try to put her at ease, which only magnified the situation. A helpless cow she was. Chewing her cud. Her gums showing, her food spilling down her lips for everyone to see.

She didn't even realize how much progress she had made delivering that afternoon until she glanced down at the last few bottles tapping against her wooden cart. The conversation with her grandfather had put her at ease about giving up Benny, but she still wondered if it were possible to make a life for herself in Damascus as her family had done for centuries. Even without Benny as her husband, the idea of life in Syria just didn't seem to fit. Even after knowing all of the dangers involved in leaving, staying still didn't feel right, no matter how many times she tried it on.

Her grandfather told her to trust her instinct. Was that too convenient for her?

A while ago, she had heard her grandfather explain Rabbi Moshe Chaim Luzatto's three-step process for making the proper decision. "First," he said, "one must search his heart to ensure that he is acting with the purist of intentions; second, one must thoroughly investigate all his options to ensure that he has done his best to properly make the right decision; and third, one must ultimately throw his burden on G-d, because 'happy is the man whose strength is in G-d'."

Was she acting with the purist of intentions? Had she done her best to make the right decision? Which way should she turn? Should she continue her search for the right boy in Syria, or was she destined to begin a life for herself someplace else, as her brothers had? It would have to come from Hashem, she decided at last. All of it - step one, step two, and step three!

Only one delivery left. She looked at the list of deliveries beside the bottles. At least she had tossed the paper into the cart. Had she relied on her memory, it probably would have failed her that day.

Her smile faded when she spotted a teenage Arab boy sitting alone outside the *hohsh* up ahead. To avoid the Arab boys who used to hang around on that street, she usually remembered to use the back alley to make her last delivery, which was just two streets down. But with all of her distracting thoughts that day, she hadn't remembered to use that route and had gone the direct way instead.

Sophia sized up the boy in a single glance. A white turban enwrapped his head, and he stared straight ahead in stony silence. The only sound that accompanied him was the unbroken rhythm of tambourines and cymbals sounding from inside the courtyard where the door to his *hohsh* hung lazily off the top hinge.

Sophia deliberated for a moment. Turning around and avoiding that street, at this point, meant walking fifteen minutes out of the way in order to reach her last delivery. And if the Arab teenager noticed her turning around, he might take that as a sign of her weakness. The last thing she needed was to get bullied by a bored Arab teenager.

She looked straight ahead, holding her head high, as if claiming her right to roam the streets at will. The bottles knocked against each other as the battered wheels teetered over the uneven street. From the corner of her eye, she could still see the boy, sitting by a stump beside the door. She ignored him and concentrated on her steering.

All at once, a gunshot blasted into the air, dispersing a group of circling pigeons.

Sophia jumped back, trying to locate the source. As she swerved around, she noticed that the Arab boy had not moved.

Another gunshot sounded, and then another, followed by cheering. She let out her breath as soon as she realized that it was probably an Armenian wedding taking place inside the *hohsh*, as it was customary to shoot in the air as part of their festivities. Quickly, she grabbed the handle of her cart and continued walking, unaware that the Arab boy had jumped off his stump and was following close behind her.

"What do you have in there?" the boy asked.

Sophia kept walking, hoping that he believed she had not heard him. "*Musawi*! Follower of Moshe!" he hollered even louder.

Anger rose up from the pit of her stomach. She took in a deep breath and realized that silence would probably bring about a more favorable outcome.

What could he want? Can't he just let me be? Maybe he wants to buy some araq *for the wedding going on,* she thought. She continued walking quickly – a step away from danger, a step away from fear, a step toward safety.

Boom! Another gunshot thundered in her ears. Her heart skipped a beat. She knew that this time, the gunshot had not come from the wedding party. She slowly turned around and spotted the Arab boy standing just two meters away from her, pointing a smoking gun into the air, but the reverberating sound was hushed by yet more gunshots coming from the wedding party inside.

People strolled by ahead on a nearby street. Only an old drunk pointed his finger in the air at the loud sound jerking him out of his inebriated state.

Should she scream? Would anyone even hear her?

Sophia held her tongue tightly between her teeth, afraid to speak. *Act normal,* she commanded herself. She stood where she was, clenching her cart's handle tightly in her trembling hands. She had heard of kidnappings in the Jewish Quarter. They were rare, but easily done.

"I said, what do you have in there?" the Arab boy repeated.

"*Araq,*" she answered finally.

"How much did you sell of that today? Give me your money!" He pointed the barrel of his gun at her.

This cannot be happening to me, she thought. *Think, Sophia, think.* When she was little, there were times when she had rehearsed this kind of scene repeatedly in her mind. Most of the time, the ending finished off with her escaping, unharmed. If she thought that the boy would leave her alone after she gave him her money, she would have offered it to him from the beginning. Somehow, she had learned differently. Giving the Arab boy a position of strength could be dangerous. To back down was a mistake. At the moment she handed over her money, she would be surrendering. Surrendering was a sign of defeat and a sign of weakness. Both might work against her, quickly.

The teenager pointed the barrel at her once more, as if trying to confirm his undeniable request. She could feel the small pouch of money that weighed down her pocket and flapped against her leg as she stepped back behind her cart, pretending to look inside for the money.

Suddenly the door to the *hohsh* behind them opened wider, revealing a guest who had just stepped out of the *hohsh*. Dressed in a three-piece suit and well-groomed, the guest stopped short at the sight of the scene he had just walked into. Then, all at once, he burst out into uncontrollable laughter. "This looks like fun," he said.

"Go back inside unless you want me to take a shot at you, too," the Arab boy said.

"Is that loaded?"

"Will you get lost? I'm trying to get some money here." He slurred his words in Arabic.

"I bet it's empty. Why don't you take a shot?"

Panic seized Sophia and she braced her entire body.

The Arab boy smiled at the suggestion, lifting his arm in an aiming position.

"Not at the *Musawi*! Don't waste bullets on her. See if you can open that bottle of *araq* for us so that we can take a drink." The Arab guest folded his arms and leaned casually beside the door.

Sophia looked over at the cart where the *araq* bottles stood, their necks clearing the top edge of the cart.

The Arab boy swaggered in an attempt to plant his feet on the ground.

Sophia stepped back against the wall of the narrow street, pressing into the wall's bumpy stones, wondering if she should recite her last Shema. *Hashem, get me out of here!*

A shot sounded from the gun, sending a bullet way into the distance.

The throbbing in her head had not missed a beat; only its pace quickened with intensity as she realized the shot had missed her.

The guest glanced down the street. "You didn't even hit the cart. What a disgrace!"

Sophia forced herself to suppress her feelings of anger and humiliation as they treated her like an object of entertainment. Her head began to spin, driven by their voices.

"That wasn't my fault. The cart moved. Did she move it?" The Arab boy turned toward her again, his gun once more pointing in her direction.

"Try again. You have nothing to lose!"

She shuddered from the shot, feeling them mocking her. At the same time, she saw her life playing before her in slow motion — her family, her home, and her future. There had to be a way to get away! Trapped between the stone wall and the corner of the cart, she saw she would have to go around the cart to escape, although running down that path would make her an even easier target.

The Arab boy stretched his arms and pulled the trigger once more, this time skimming the cart's wheel.

"Keep going!" The Arab guest cheered him on, and the boy did - again and again and again, cackling and snorting in between shots.

Sophia's stomach twisted tighter and tighter like a rubber cord about to snap.

"Higher! Lower! Keep your eye on your target!" the guest instructed the boy. Sophia's eye caught a glimpse of the amusing grin on the young Arab man's face as he uttered each command, and she thought she would go out of her mind just from the blasts vibrating in her ears. She flattened her body against the wall, wishing that she could just evaporate.

As the boy pulled the trigger again, the weapon made a faint *click*, revealing an empty handgun. Before she could look up, the Arab guest had already jumped on the boy, pinning him to the ground. He lifted his head to Sophia and shouted, "Run!"

Shock overwhelmed her. She hesitated for a second as the boy writhed beneath the weight of the Arab guest.

"Run! Go!" he yelled. His arresting eyes confirmed his tone.

That's when she sprinted past the cart, skimming a piece of protruding wood. She looked down at her cut ankle, hopping from the stinging sensation. Then she ran and didn't look back. Her skirts flew behind her, their delicate white layers fluttering in the wind. She gasped for air, the sounds of her erratic panting and pounding footsteps in a constant rhythm. The stinging pain faded each time her numb feet hit the stone ground. When she swirled her head around to see if anyone was behind her, the tight braid that ran down her back whipped her face.

Sophia stopped to take a gulp of air, heaving quick breaths that didn't even feel like they were helping. She pressed her hand on her pulsating ankle where the cart had sliced into it, and then continued sprinting. Halfway through the Jewish Quarter, the Arab guest's deep brown eyes flashed before her — in the window of the next *hohsh*, in the distance of the setting sun, at the pastry shop, and in the crowds she passed, screaming, "Run!"

11

When Sophia stormed into the house, Huda was dumping leftover food over the railing of the front steps. Not a sound quivered inside. She tore past the dirty dinner dishes, racing down the hall. The deafening rounds of the firing gun haunted her mind.

"Ma? Mother!" she screamed.

Suddenly, she stopped, remembering for the first time that she had left her cart at the Arab boy's home. Everyone at the *souk* knew that was Grandpa Yosef's *araq* inside. Now that boy would know how to find her. Now he would know where she lived. The Arab guest would also know it. Sophia didn't trust him, either. Why would the Arab guest call her a *Musawi*, mock her, and then turn around to help her?

"Mother? Father?" she screamed again, unable to contain her fear of being alone a single moment longer.

Her mother's footsteps came up the stairs. "I was just at Boomeh. I was beginning to worry."

"I'm leaving!" Sophia slammed the door behind them.

"What are you saying? Where were you?"

Sophia paced the floor. "I'm leaving Syria. I can't stay here another minute." She ran into the kitchen and pulled a green bottle off the shelf. Steadying her foot on a chair, she struggled with the cap and poured the brownish-red liquid on her cut. "Oww!" She squeezed her eyes tightly in pain.

Her mother watched the medicine drip onto the white stone floor. "Sophia, what are you doing? Are you alright?"

"No, I am not alright! I cut my leg trying to run away from a lunatic who used my *araq* as target practice. I felt like a hostage. He wouldn't stop shooting. I made it home, but now he has our cart and probably knows where we live."

"Here, let me help you."

The front door banged against its frame.

Sophia jumped up.

Her mother lifted the spilling bottle. "Shlomo?" she called out to her husband, her quivering voice marked with desperation.

Her father's footsteps sounded in the hallway. "Yes?"

Sophia dropped into her chair, huffing at her own panic.

"She's home. We're in here, Shlomo."

Sophia's father stopped short in the doorway and stared at them both. "What is going on here? I have been looking all over for you, Sophia !"

"Someone threatened her with a gun ... her leg is cut."

Her father stepped in closer. "Sophia?" He put on his glasses and leaned over to see the laceration. "It doesn't look too bad. Your skin has scraped off, and the cut looks more long than deep. Let's clean it well and cover it gently."

"I'll get the ointment," Rose offered.

"Where did this happen?" her father asked.

"Outside an Armenian *hohsh* at the end of the Jewish Quarter. It was my fault. I should have gone around the back way like I usually do. By the time I realized that, it was too late. He demanded that I give him all my money—"

"Who did?"

"Some boy from the party. He kept shooting his gun. No one heard him because they were shooting from inside the *hohsh*, too ... for a wedding or something."

Rose stepped in with some supplies. She gently straightened Sophia's leg on a stool and cleaned it once more before she applied the ointment and bandaged it.

Sophia closed her eyes and leaned her head back, battling to erase the sounds of the gunshots that were still reverberating inside her.

"How do you feel?"

"I don't know!" Sophia snapped. She heaved a sigh big enough to hold every emotion she had felt that day. "I thought that I would never see my family again." She looked up at her parents. The hostile tone that she had used before now sat wedged in her throat. She took a few rapid breaths, and then the breaths gradually broke up, allowing the sobs to take over. She bent over crying, her face hidden in her hands.

Shlomo Zalta shook out a handkerchief from his waist pocket and handed it to her. "You'll be fine, young lady. Just fine," he said, patting her arm lightly.

Her parents spared her the long speech about walking alone in the streets of Damascus. She attributed their kindness to the shock that overcame them each time they witnessed the rare occasion when she broke down and cried.

✶ ✶ ✶

Sophia tossed and turned in her bed, her covers lying on the floor beside her. The bit of sleep that she did get wavered with the pain of her throbbing leg. She was almost thankful for that pain. Her pain kept her mind from dreaming.

Their faces flashed before her over and over again. The smiling, mocking face of the Arab boy forcing her to look at him. She could see him cackling and snorting, calling her *Musawi*. The Arab guest called her *Musawi*. He encouraged the Arab boy to shoot the gun, pushing him to release all the bullets, and then jumped on him. For what? She would never know.

Suddenly, she remembered her request to Hashem that afternoon. Was this part of His response?

She threw her legs over her bed and pried the window open with both hands. The window hook swung off the latch. She sat in silence. Impatient clouds rushed across the sky, providing her with a momentary breeze which touched her through the open panes. Three rows of geometric designs trimmed the wall beneath her window, running across all the walls of her house. Different variations of the same design framed arches over the rest of the doorways and niches that filled the courtyard of black, yellow, red, and white stones. But their vibrant colors had long since cracked and faded, just as the rest of Damascus, which stood in a state of disrepair.

She stared at the designs, wondering if her life would be the same – cracked, faded, and destined for Damascus.

A vision of her brothers intruded on her thoughts. She could see them running around the trees, trampling the roots which grew from a mound of dirt encircled by the stone courtyard. She wondered about the life they were now living – a life she could never have. "Well, why not?" she asked herself, slamming the window shut.

She continued in a mocking voice, "Because they had maps – detailed drawings of their escape routes – opportunities that you, Sophia, do not have!"

Maps. Did they take them? What if they were searched? Wouldn't they leave them home?

She slipped into a chair and dozed off, as a voice inside her head continued whispering, "The map, the map, the map…" until she woke up in a sweat an hour later with the word "map" on her lips.

Suddenly, an idea challenged her intuition. Half the night she lay awake, wondering if she was right. She had all night to think, to plan. If she was right, somehow she would convince her father to arrange for her escape from Syria – even if it meant going alone.

She thought about running to the cellar to confirm her suspicions, but was held back by the melodies of nocturnal insects and birds of prey sounding out in the darkness of the night. Twice, she glanced out the window which offered a clear view of the door to their *hohsh*. The *hohsh* stood bolted as it did each night, but the cart did not sit along the wall in its usual spot.

An orange glow crept up the sky, introducing daylight. Sophia pulled her hair into a knot and yanked on Gazeem's old gardening boots before dashing through the courtyard. She jumped out into the courtyard where Gazeem was wrestling with a dead trunk using his bare hands.

"Did you see the cart, Gazeem?" she asked him.

"Not this morning, Miss." He rocked the trunk from side to side and rubbed his weathered hands on the sides of his pants before giving the trunk one final heave. The dirt pulled up with the trunk and the roots cracked beneath while he tilted it to one side and sliced the remainder of the stubborn roots with his knife.

She pressed her hands against either side of the doorframe and looked up and down the street outside her *hohsh*. No pushcart.

Sophia swung open the door to the cellar, peering at the steps below for any slithering company. Then she ran down and yanked on the string dangling from the ceiling until the light bulb went on. She frantically moved her hands along the floor, wedging dirt and sand under her fingernails. She pushed the vat from the wall, squeezing her way through. It was gone. Gone.

She fell back on the stone floor and stared into the darkness. Then she looked hesitantly over her shoulder. She remembered putting it behind the vat. No one walked down those steps except for her and, from time to time, Grandpa Yosef.

Who was down here? Sophia stood quickly, stamping her feet to shake off the cold feeling from them, and looked over her shoulder once more. She tilted the dangling light bulb overhead so that a flash of light darted along the cellar floor behind her. Maybe Boomeh had organized the cellar to surprise Sophia, like she sometimes organized the house to surprise her mother. Whenever Boomeh finished such jobs, the entire house seemed to lie in rows of order.

"It's not that neat down here." Sophia's voice echoed in the cellar, even though it was just above a whisper. She released the bulb and faced the vat, eyeing its placement. Then, for the first time, she noticed it – sticking out from under the vat. *Was that where she had moved it?* She reached down and tugged. Out came the cardboard she had hid. Sophia fingered the red, grimy lines and markings of the drawing, trying to follow their beginnings and their ends.

All at once, it hit her like the start of a hurricane, steady and unwavering, telling her that quick acceptance was safer than standing at the shore in denial. She stared at the drawing a minute longer, digesting the truth of her discovery. Her hands gripped onto what her brothers, Ezra and Yosef, had used to escape Syria – maybe what the *Mukhabarat* had been searching for. She trembled while clinging to the single drawing that could make the difference between life and death. And it was she who had stumbled upon it while it collected dust in the dark cellar.

She looked above at the closed cellar door, making certain that no one was watching. Then, she sprang straight up and jumped into the air, first softly and then as high as she could, with the cardboard still in her grasp, thinking that she had never laughed so hard before. When she stopped to catch her breath, she lifted the drawing to her lips and kissed it.

She reached for a nearby ladder and slammed it against the wall where a portion of the torn ceiling revealed wooden beams stacked up in rows. Then she stuck the cardboard in between the wooden beams and the floor of the room above, pressing the cardboard corners and camouflaging them in the tattered ceiling. The beams stood almost as close as the shoots of bamboo, which formed the roof of her family's sukkah each year. Only, no stars peeked between them in the cellar. No moon shone through. No air escaped.

"The map," she whispered, still afraid to say the words out loud. Dark notions began to creep into her mind, yet she pushed those discouraging thoughts away, refusing to diminish the thrilling feeling of her dream. Thoughts of leaving her family and never seeing them again, thoughts of their safety as well as her own, and thoughts marked by a nagging fear of failure - all stood halted by her screaming, trilling hopes.

She pressed her hand against her heart. "Thank you, Hashem." Her voice carried through the musty air, echoing against the sandy stones.

12

That evening, the September sun slipped down and tucked itself into a pocket of haze just above the top edge of the *hohsh* wall. Unlike other courtyards in the old city of Damascus which held an outer court for receiving guests and an inner court for the family, Sophia's family's *hohsh* held one courtyard shared by everyone. No one really counted the small courtyard off the back alley, originally intended to make room for the servants and services, although it did come in handy to mask the hanging laundry and the messy preparations for Boomeh's wedding.

Sophia stepped along the black, white, and yellow stones that graced the floors in an alternating pattern that boasted of Mamluk influence from the thirteenth century[1]. Her footsteps echoed across the faded designs of the stones.

---

1 The Mamluk Dynasty ruled in Damascus, Syria from 1260-1516.

For the third time that day, she opened the door to her *hohsh*, peering down the street. No sign of her cart. Just the darkness silently creeping into the late hour. She slammed the door.

In front of the walled staircase, shaded under a tree, Grandpa Yosef sat, his eyes closed, resting the back of his head against the cold stone topped by a laced iron railing overhead. The uninterrupted sound of birds rose in unison.

When Rose Zalta had married, her father had insisted that the bride and groom move into his house. Separate apartments joined together in a *hohsh* ensured privacy. It was not unusual for several families to live together in this way for many generations. Somehow, Sophia's grandfather made his son-in-law feel like it was his *hohsh*, and in turn, her father took over the responsibilities incumbent upon him.

Short creases formed in the vest Grandpa wore beneath his suit jacket, where an open book rested on its pages over his stomach. Sophia approached him, quickening her step as she reached the stairs to her house.

"*Araq* to honor the New Year?" her grandfather commented, his eyes still closed.

Sophia looked down at the wrapped bottle of *araq* in her hand. "Actually, to put Father in a good mood."

He opened his eyes halfway, his blonde lashes framing sky-blue eyes. "There is nothing as sweet as the truth. I believe you will achieve both – sweetness and truth." He smiled before closing his eyes again.

Sophia lifted her chin. "Thank you, Grandpa."

The door to the house swung open and Huda, dressed in her usual black *chador* with veil, began her ritual of sweeping the steps, starting at the bottom and working her way up so that each step always carried the dirt from the ones above it.

Sophia stepped around a bony black cat sitting on the top step and opened the door.

At the dinner table later that night, Sophia's mother whispered to her husband, "Really, Shlomo. It wouldn't be so terrible if we hired a new maid. I just can't take her ways. She just can't seem to pick up a routine, and I've tried. Believe me, I've tried."

"Maybe we should offer to keep the cat," Sophia said.

"I doubt that she would mind it if we did," Rose said. "She tortures that poor animal. Sometimes I wonder why she even bothers with that cat."

Jack handed his plate to Boomeh to fill with food.

Sophia's father lifted his plate above a bowl of *bameh* while his wife scooped a heap of rice onto it. "At least she doesn't steal," he said.

"That's because in Saudi Arabia they'd chop off your hand first," Sophia said, before biting into a *keftes*.

"Really?" Boomeh asked.

Jack slid his glasses up his nose. "How do you know such things?"

Grandpa Yosef closed his eyes.

Her father mumbled something to himself as he set down his plate.

Sophia brought her father the *araq* from the curio

cabinet. "Grandfather's latest. I taste—" Sophia stopped herself short. Her comment went unnoticed by everyone except for Boomeh, who looked on with clear disapproval.

"Ahh," Shlomo said, before wrestling with the cork. An amber glow flickered through the bottle from the candles her mother lit every night to elevate the souls of the great *tzaddikim*. He poured the clear liquid into his glass.

Sophia snuck a peek at her grandfather.

"A slew of boys were born to the Arab community this month," her father continued before poking his fork into a drumstick coated with soft apricots. "Hardly a girl in the bunch. You'll never guess why." He sniffed the aroma rising from the glass of *araq*, then looked up at everyone.

"Grandpa's *araq*?" Rose asked in disbelief.

"Yes, it's the talk of the *souk*. I gave out *araq* to some of the neighbors and merchants I know. They are convinced that Grandfather's *araq* brings sons to all the men who drink it. I have requests for ten dozen cases. I assured them that we have no intention of turning this into a family business, but there are some who practically followed me all the way home. They are willing to pay four times the price of regular *araq*."

Jack smacked his forehead. "*Beje'nen* – unbelievable!"

Boomeh arranged her own plate, tilting the chicken juices to one side to ensure that they didn't touch the rice.

Now was Sophia's chance. She sat up in her chair, waiting to jump in.

"Another one of my friends left school last week," Sophia blurted out.

"It is not safe to speak about these matters," her father said sternly.

"They are safe, though, in the Aretz." Sophia bit down so hard on the *keftes* that she bit her fork, too. Her mouth vibrated when the metal tines clashed with her teeth.

Sophia's father wiped his lips firmly with a napkin. In a matter of seconds, the color red flushed his cheeks. "Even if the *Mukhabarat* did not figure out what your friend is up to and she did manage to escape, that is not the end. I hope that her family does not have to pay a deadly price for this child's happiness."

Sophia's fork shook in her hand. "So this is the life which you want for me?"

Shlomo Zalta pushed his chair away from the table. "And what is so wrong with that—"

"Pharaoh is coming," Jack mumbled, helping himself to another serving of rice.

Huda dragged herself down the hall. They all waited until she closed the front door behind her.

"You never know," said Jack. "Even Jews are informing on each other. You can't be careful enough around here."

Sophia detected a look of disgust on her father's face and hoped it was aimed at Jack.

Rose Zalta brushed her hands on her apron in a downward motion - down, down, down, as if attempting to smooth out the wrinkles in the conversation.

Shlomo peered at his daughter. "Young lady, you started going out already. I thought that you were past these ideas, or has all this just been a game to you?" He flung down his napkin beside his plate.

Sophia stared at her father, and everything she had planned to say to him stuck in her throat.

Rose gently patted her daughter's hand. "Sophia, look at your sister Boomeh. She is very happy. She is married and will soon start a family."

"A big one!" Jack said.

"With G-d's help, you will also have the same happiness here in Syria. We are here for you. We can help you, and you can live with us. Won't that be nice?" Sophia's mother saw her daughter's uneasiness. "There are Jews all over the world with problems, Sophia. Not being able to travel freely is just something we have learned to accept."

"As you will," her father added.

Sophia rubbed her eyes, her thoughts writhing for territory. *No! I can't! I won't. How can you call this a normal life for us? How can you subjugate yourself to them and the life they have defined for you? The* Mukhabarat, *Assad, and all those who lurk in the darkness to trip us up so that we may experience the ultimate tortures. I can't survive another day of it!*

"There aren't any other choices," Boomeh said.

Sophia rolled a bitten *keftes* around in circles, scooping up the extra sauce on her plate. With each circle, she remembered her conversation with Eva and her opinions about their lack of choices. With each circle, she collected her perseverance and her strength. "It worked for my brothers. What if I wanted the same life for myself in the Aretz on holy soil? What would be so terrible?"

Shlomo's voice dropped to a whisper. "Your brothers had detailed routes to travel by. No one has been able to find copies of those routes again. The *Mukhabarat* has been looking the hardest. They have already warned us that discovering such a thing in the hands of a Jew will cause immediate hanging, publicly, in the middle of the city's square for everyone to see."

"For everyone to fear," Grandpa Yosef added.

"What if I was able to find that route? The same route that my brothers used."

Jack slumped in his chair. "What is she talking about now?"

Boomeh pursed her lips and nodded loyally at her husband's comment.

"Your brothers … *that* was a long time ago," her father said, a distant look in his eyes.

"Four years ago," Grandpa said.

Her father took a deep breath. "Ezra and Yosef escaped before the Yom Kippur War. It's only one year after the war, and we are still suffering the after-effects of Israel's victory. Security is tighter now than ever. Like I said, discovering escape routes out of Syria is top priority for the Syrian government. There is even talk about instituting a night curfew in the Jewish Quarter. The moles and sleepers planted by the *Mukhabarat* are now being called upon for duty."

Grandpa Yosef cleared his throat. "As our sages tell us, 'The salvation of Hashem comes in the blink of an eye.'"

Sophia reached behind the bookcase and pulled out the cardboard she had brought up from the cellar. She handed it to her father. Everyone fell silent. Jack held his hand over his mouth in disbelief.

Shlomo studied the drawing for a moment and then a smile came over his face. "You think you're smart, huh?

You have finally found what you were looking for – your ticket out of Syria."

Sophia frowned at her father's sarcasm. The deep lines contouring beneath her cheekbones angled all the way to her lips. Her stare faded everything around her except for him.

Shlomo threw the cardboard back at his daughter. "This is nothing! You've found a nursery drawing that one of your brothers probably colored in the fourth grade."

Sophia stepped back, as if inching away from one of the snakes in the cellar, and dropped the drawing by her father's chair. Only it was shame and not fear which caused her to do so.

Rose pulled her daughter to sit beside her. "Sophia, sweetie," she said, hissing through her teeth, "there are details you don't know about. Details ... we chose not to share with you. Your brothers' escape, although, *baruch* Hashem, successful, did not go unnoticed by the *Mukhabarat*." She looked up at her husband. A single tear fell down her cheek.

Jack looked over at Boomeh. Boomeh's stare was fixed on her mother's hands clenched in her lap.

"I have a hard enough time getting a job to support this family, and then I have to listen to this, too? That is enough!" Sophia's father bellowed. "I don't want to hear another word about it!"

Sophia slammed her hands down on the table as she stood up. Then she stomped off to her room, her footsteps causing each crystal drop in the chandelier to quiver over everyone's heads as they finished eating in silence.

13

The next morning Sophia found herself in the same splintered bed with the same ill feeling she fell asleep with the night before. She slipped into Gazeem's gardening boots and pulled on a dress long enough to cover her pajamas. On her way out, she grabbed half the money from her knitted purse and stuffed it into her dress pocket.

A young man entered the courtyard carrying a *sefer* and looking for her grandfather.

"My rabbi sent me to ask him a question. Is that, umm, alright?"

Sophia ushered the man inside and went to call her grandfather, who had just settled down for his morning routine of learning.

Once back outside, Sophia scanned the courtyard from the top of the steps. No cart. She pulled on the door to her *hohsh*. No cart on the street, either. She stepped onto the street and closed the door with a thump.

Wet fur rubbed against her leg, spiking her flesh. "Meow," a muddy cat whined.

She jumped back. The cat squirmed away, abandoning a shivering bird it had trapped against the wall. Sophia cupped her hands, picked up the small dove, and hurled it up to the sky, watching it soar to freedom.

She set out on her weekly routine of giving charity before Shabbat. She looked up to identify the home of the widow to whom she gave money each week and quickly slipped some loose coins into an apron hanging to dry outside the woman's door. Sophia had watched her grandfather giving charity that way and had learned from him to always give the money quietly, on her own and to never speak of the recipients.

Her grandfather once told her that the world was charged with a specific spiritual energy on Rosh Hashanah, the same energy each year, dating back to the time of Creation. The month of Elul was always spent in preparation for the new year. She looked up at the sky, searching for the newness, purity, truth, and Divine assistance that her grandfather had spoken of, wondering if she was worthy of any of it. What kind of life would be decided for her this year? In which book would the Heavenly Courts inscribe her?

Have I faithfully become the best I can be, fulfilling my mission in life? But then, what is my mission? Where is my mission?

Several more steps and a turn brought her to another neighbor's *hohsh*, where she stuffed more liras into robes and pants. She was gaining inside, as her pockets emptied. Giving without seeing, without comforting, without speaking – that was how she gave her charity each week.

It was late morning when she returned home with a handful of fresh figs from the market. Boomeh's framed needlepoint hung crooked on the wall in the front hall – flowers arranged in a vase, the pattern of woolen yarn woven by a skilled hand, perfect in its crookedness. Sophia straightened the frame as it hung over her head, its calm colors smooth under her fingertips, its beginning chaotic, never anticipating the beauty of its completion. The straight rows of color set in a pattern like the life she saw in front of her, the life they all expected her to lead. She tilted the corner of the frame back to where she had found it, much preferring its crookedness.

Sophia set the figs down on her bedroom dresser. She untied a bag of dried fruit from the top drawer to see how much she had managed to collect over the past few weeks. The dried preserves was her idea of fast, easy food for traveling, just in case the need arose, just in case the opportunity to leave Syria came her way, just in case, just in case.

Boomeh snuck up behind her. "*What* are you doing?"

"Nothing." Sophia yanked the sack behind her back.

"What are you hiding?" Boomeh struggled to see.

Sophia jumped onto her bed and stuffed the bag under her blanket. "Why can't you leave me alone?" Sophia cried.

"Why can't you just show me quietly what you've got?" Boomeh pulled at the blanket.

"I won't!"

"I'm older," Boomeh commanded.

"Don't, Boomeh, don't!" Sophia wrestled the covers from her sister's grip.

"Sit still then and show me."

"All right, all right!" Sophia said. "Sit back."

When Boomeh did, Sophia lifted the covers, threw them over Boomeh's head, and sprinted out of the room with the sack. She ran through the front room, catching a glimpse of her father, at the last second, who was walking toward her. Before she could stop herself, she had rammed right into him.

"Sophia?"

"Are you alright, Father? Sorry." She grabbed her father's *tarboosh* that had fallen to the floor and handed it to him. Then she dropped her sack into her pocket before Boomeh could return.

Shlomo Zalta pressed his hat over his head. "You are going to have to slow down eventually, young lady! And it cannot happen soon enough."

Sophia shrank back.

"Now, where were you this morning?" her father asked, absently arranging some bottles he had on the table.

"Just out for a walk."

"Alone?"

The question hit her with all of its heaviness. She had never imagined that one word was able to question the trust she'd always thought her father had in her. "What are those bottles for?" she asked him, in an attempt to change the uncomfortable subject.

"They are for business."

"A new business?"

"Yes, as a pharmacist's assistant. I would like to get started so that I can fill all of these orders of merchandise."

"Wow." Sophia sat down next to him and picked up one of the brown bottles marked 'chamomile'. "What's this one for?"

"It is apparently an herb used to calm patients, basically a painkiller. Mr. Hakim bought a couple as samples to see how they would go, even though most of his business consists of drugs and chemicals."

"Okay. Good luck." Sophia pushed back her chair, beginning to rise.

"Not so fast, young lady. There are some things that I would like to discuss with you."

She set down the chamomile bottle she had been holding and dropped back into her chair, feeling the severity in his words.

"I know that your grades are at the top of your class. But I have decided that your schooling is no longer appropriate for you. You are sixteen now."

"My friends go to school. What is so bad about school?" Sophia asked.

"The secular Jews of France have managed to convince some to adopt their new modern culture. They opened up schools here in Sham and Halab with their "dignified" ideas, congratulating themselves on educating their Middle Eastern brethren. As it is, they have flooded the curriculum with everything except for what you should be learning. We already have a *mesorah* passed down to us by Moshe Rabeinu. It is an order of purity and truth. We have enough of a responsibility keeping to our own order. We don't have to adopt someone else's."

"But Father, we will always have our tradition. Why does that have to change?"

"Everything we do and see and read affects our tradition. I don't care how alone I stand on this matter. My daughter will not be a part of it."

"No school?"

"You'll do just fine."

"But what *will* I do?"

"Now that you will be having more free time on your hands," he said, ignoring her question, "I do not want you traveling alone anymore."

"But I wasn't traveling."

"You are right. Let me re-phrase that." Shlomo leaned in closer so that she could see the creases in his forehead. "I do not want you leaving this house anymore without an escort. Do you understand?"

Sophia nodded, sinking deeper into her chair.

"That will put a stop to your *araq* deliveries," he said with a sideways glance. "Oh, and one more thing: I have offered your services as a midwife's apprentice to help your mother on the calls she has been getting."

"Babies? I don't know a thing about delivering babies!"

"You don't need to. Helping out with the supplies is probably all the assistance your mother needs. And it might be a way for you to keep busy, at least until you find a suitable husband."

Sophia dropped her head backward until it hit the top of the chair.

Shlomo Zalta slid a green book in front of her. "Why don't you take this? It's about all of the natural remedies you seemed so interested in."

No school! No araq! *No walks! Midwife's apprentice?!* Sophia closed the door to her room and tossed the green book onto her bed. What was her life coming to? She flopped down on her bed, only it didn't bounce back up the way it used to. It had been a while since the man with the brass rods came to fluff up her cotton mattress. This time, the mattress smacked her in the stomach as if she did a belly-flop on the lake. Her eyes popped open from the shock of the pain.

Babies?! What would she do with babies?

* * *

There was no time to think her way out of it. The neighbor two streets down stood at the Zaltas' front door, her fists banging between the iron bars. "I came for Rose. My neighbor is having a baby!" the woman said. "Is Mrs. Zalta here?"

Sophia followed closely behind her mother and the frail woman, keeping up with their quick strides. The dark streets of Damascus were bare except for the occasional merchant sleeping by his wagon at the corner of the road.

They heard yelling outside the *hohsh*. "We better hurry," the woman said.

Rose whispered in her daughter's ear before they entered the doorway, "I don't expect anything from you tonight, Sophia. Let's just see how it goes, okay?"

"Sure," Sophia said in as steady a voice as she could

muster. She said it with her scrubbed face, hair slicked back into a bun, and crisp white shirt tucked into a freshly laundered skirt, while in her hands she clutched a small book of Tehillim.

They knocked and opened the front door just as a clay jug whisked by them and smashed into the wall.

Rose lurched backward into Sophia. Inside the apartment, a man at the far end of the room had ducked in time, but the expectant mother kept after him. "I don't want any help, I told you! Just go!"

The frail woman whispered from the steps, "Rose, I can't come in. I have to tend to my children." And with that, she was already off, releasing them from her grip as quickly as she had snatched them up.

Sophia closed the door behind them.

"Tunie, calm down!" The man had his hands out as if to catch any more obstacles that could be thrown his way.

"I'll take over from here," Sophia's mother said, stepping forward in a way that Sophia had never seen before. She walked up to the couple and unsnapped her bag. "I'm Rose. I'm in charge now. This here," she motioned to her daughter, "is Sophia. We work together." Sophia smiled and nodded.

"Are you the lucky father?" Rose asked the young man who was perspiring and had creases of fear etched onto his face.

The man nodded, not up, just down. Down. Down. Down – as if he was unable to lift his chin.

"Well, *mabruk* – congratulations - to you! Let's give this beautiful wife of yours some space to do her job. You have time for a nice walk; maybe visit the *bet midrash* down the block. I think the fresh air would do you some good."

He looked at his wife, who had been staring at Sophia's mother since she walked in.

"Is that okay with you?" Rose asked her, handing a handkerchief to Tunie's husband.

Tunie let out a deep breath. "Just make sure you stay in the *bet midrash* so we know where to find you."

"Whatever makes you happy, dear. I will be at the *bet midrash*, then ... right down the block ... praying," he said, already halfway out the door.

"Bye," his wife called after him.

Rose took Tunie by the arm. "Let's get to work, young lady." Together, they stepped over the scattered pieces of the clay jug. Rose looked back at her daughter.

Already, Sophia had grabbed a broom from the corner and begun sweeping.

Rose smiled. "Sophia, I'm glad you are here," she said before entering the bedroom off the hall.

The door was almost closed, but she heard them talking – her mother's voice coaching, counting down the minutes until the baby came, pulling the seconds from time, and encouraging another soul to join them.

Meanwhile, Sophia had swept every corner, slipped every book back into place, cleaned the pots and dishes, and stacked them on the shelf. She had even opened her book of Tehillim once or twice, but her eyes closed on their own and she dozed off in a chair until morning.

A wail broke into the silence. Sophia jumped out of the chair, searching around frantically for the source of the sudden and loud noise. Was a train passing close by? She didn't see any lights flashing outside. The only thing shining back at her were the pots she had scoured and stacked on the shelf.

The wailing continued, stronger and clearer now. *The baby!* Sophia rushed to the basin and washed her hands and face. She ran toward the room that her mother had stepped into hours earlier. The door was still closed. Quickly, she raised her hand to knock, then stopped her knuckles short of the door, slowing them down to a soft tap.

"Sophia?" her mother called.

"Yes. I'm here if you need me. I've washed up."

Rose Zalta brought out the baby wrapped in a white sheet. His arms and legs were wrapped up just enough to quiet him down. "It's a boy," Rose said, her voice huskier than the night before, her face weathered and glowing, as if she had had the child herself. She placed the baby in Sophia's arms. "Hold him, Sophia. I have to go to fetch his father."

"How is Tunie?"

"She is resting. Just hold the baby. He is just as tired as his mother and shouldn't give you much trouble now. I'll be back soon."

Sophia's arms locked into a cradle, and she rocked the newborn gently. Lighter than a bottle of *araq*, he squirmed and then eased himself back into her arms. For a few seconds, he opened his eyes. Through his slate blue stare she saw a pure soul looking back at her, his silky fingers curling over his face. She slipped her pinky through his grip. "A life given so easily, Hashem ... with such perfection. How do You do it?" she couldn't help saying out loud.

She peeked into the bedroom. Tunie had fallen asleep. Darkness faded. The shadows in the bedroom took form as the beginnings of dawn ushered in the sun.

Sophia could feel the muscles in her back tightening together, like a net of wet ropes after it dried and shrank down to size. She arched her back slightly, but it didn't give. *Some things are worth the wait,* she thought. All it took was time - time to wait for the miracle to occur.

She thought about miracles more in the morning, walking back home with her mother with the sweat of dew clinging to the soles of her shoes. Did she look at all of Hashem's creations as fresh miracles each day? Did she appreciate them properly? Did she swipe her fingers through the dew at dawn? Did she wait for the sun every morning, faithfully? Did she duck from the clouds, hoping they wouldn't fall to the ground? She had skipped countless times past the oranges and dates hanging from the trees outside her window, yet had never marveled at their growth - fed by the sun, about one hundred and fifty million kilometers away. Eating each delicious one was truly like eating the sun!

Yet, unlike fruit, man was G-d's ultimate creation, able to change the world. But how could *she* possibly change the world? How could anyone change the world confined to a life in Syria, in Damascus, in the defined borders of the Jewish Quarter – no different than an orange or a date? At least in the Aretz, when people yearned for change and growth and purpose, there, they could accomplish these goals in freedom.

Sophia spotted Grandpa Yosef in the courtyard, reading - confined to the Jewish Quarter, to the house, to his chair! Somehow, though, she knew that the world was a better place with him, because of him, because of his Torah, his wisdom, his light.

Sophia went straight to her room. As she slept, someone walked in to surprise the rest of the family with news good enough to make her father whistle through the house all day long.

14

Boomeh was expecting a baby. Jack had a hard time containing his excitement until he received good wishes from the entire Jewish Quarter.

Sophia had noticed Boomeh looking a little sluggish. That afternoon, she watched from the window as Huda's black cat jumped into the small puddles of sudsy water that spilled out of the clothes-basin beside Huda. The Saudi housekeeper dunked the clothing into the water and wrung each piece dry. As she did so, the cat licked the drops of water dripping from her black sleeves.

Boomeh walked around the mess, the news of her expectance evident from the apron tied around her waist. In anticipation of the baby, Jack had cleared out the old furniture in their apartment and had given the walls a fresh coat of paint. Sophia watched Boomeh's life form before her eyes – married, baby, Damascus … trapped!

Her father stepped beside her. "What are you staring at?"

"Trapped," Sophia said, leaning her forehead against the cool pane. Then she pulled her head away from the window. "I mean ... I mean ..."

Her father arched his brow, biting on an empty pipe. "I'll be leaving for the pharmacy soon. I could use your help with the inventory."

Several gates marked the entrances to the old city of Damascus. Outside the *Haret al-Yehoud*, the gate of Bab Touma stood in the middle of a bustling intersection where cars, herded cattle, and swearing taxi drivers fought for their territory. There began the road to Bab Sharqi, where Sophia and her father continued on foot. The market stretched all the way up Bab Sharqi Street. It stretched with sacks of potatoes, nuts, and zucchini; with red and purple tapestries swinging over mother-of-pearl inlay and brass dishes holding flavored tobacco; with turquoise beaded scarves and embroidered handkerchiefs waving in the air; and with pumpkin seeds and corn hair glistening in the sunlight outside Mr. Hakim's shop. A cup of goat's milk sat on a stool at the entrance. Several bugs floated on top. Shlomo Zalta walked by the open store. "Hakim?" he called softly.

Sophia knew what her father was thinking. A man never left his stall unless he closed up first. Nothing stirred from inside.

Her father switched on the lamp beside Mr. Hakim's desk where his pharmaceutical license hung low. White bottles and small boxes with different labels covered most of the shelves and in a corner, essential oils in brown bottles released several different scents, although that of cinnamon hit Sophia as being strongest.

Many people came by that day. "We're just going to have to help them until Mr. Hakim gets here. Where is he?" Shlomo muttered, shaking his head.

Sophia spent most of the day filling up bottles with a funnel and counting tablets as her father instructed her. "When it comes to people's medicine, there is no room for error. Count them twice." And she did. Just about every drug said, "Made in Syria". Mr. Hakim didn't even have to import the better drugs from France. A new factory opened in Syria, bringing with it a more generous supply to go around, just at the right opportunity. Mr. Hakim thanked Hashem that he didn't have to entertain the idea of acquiring drugs from France, especially since the French ones demanded a higher price and since most of those contacts were made through the black market.

Without a license, her father was only able to fill out the orders that Mr. Hakim had approved. The rest of the crowd looking to order their prescriptions were sent home until Mr. Hakim returned.

When it was quiet, her father allowed her to sample the different oils and read up on their corresponding ailments. She learned that chamomile calms, tea tree disinfects, lemon invigorates, and clove warms. She also found out that ginger alleviates nausea and eucalyptus heals coughs. When her father offered to pay her, she asked for a few samples of the oils instead. Sophia finished packing some samples in smaller bottles and stuffed them into her small bag as she waited for her father to lock up the cabinets at the end of the day.

Her father looked around the market one last time for Hakim. Sophia began to pull down the metal gate over the storefront.

"Don't trouble yourself with that," her father said, hurrying to help her.

"I can do it, Father," she said, ignoring his protective way.

They passed the crossroad after Bab al-Saghir, also known as "The Little Gate". That was where the vaulted arcades and majestic trees adorning Khan al-Zait, the warehouse of olive oil, slowly came into view.

Sophia looked up at the arched ceilings in the enclosed courtyard. "Four hundred years old," her father said, following her stare. "My father used to take me here when I was a little boy. It was the only place he would buy his oil."

Her father exchanged a few words with an Arab in a green checkered headdress. When they finished talking, Sophia and her father left the olive oil warehouse without the oil they had come to buy. They walked opposite Bab al-Jabiye to avoid the entrance to Souk Midhat Pasha. Many fights had broken out among the sacks and mounds of garments there. Mostly Bedouins covered the street, struggling to find a bargain at the second-hand clothes market.

Past the Turkish baths and before the gold market, perfume sellers traded their fragrances. Shlomo Zalta walked right up to the busiest one, on the corner of al-

Bzouriye Street. "This one is known for his authentic and long-lasting perfumes. People also come for his modest prices," he told Sophia.

Sophia waited outside while her father spoke to the man in the back. After a few minutes, her father came out, without any perfume. Sophia followed him, looking back at the man in the shop. "I don't understand, Father."

"Understand what?"

She looked back at the man again and then at her father. "You walk in, you talk, and then you walk out with nothing. I thought we were buying."

Her father walked beside her without speaking about the secret thoughts and clandestine deeds of their classified life. But she knew they existed. They all knew.

They turned the next corner in the Jewish Quarter. "Mr. Hakim's *hohsh* is off the street at the south end of the *haret*," her father said.

Before her father could stop at the door to his *hohsh*, Sophia placed her hand on his elbow, keeping up her even pace. When he turned to her, her eyes revealed her discovery. Two men hovered at the next corner in plainclothes, wearing thin and tapered mustaches. She smiled at him and mumbled the words, "Keep walking, Father."

Fear rose up inside her. Her father smiled at her as they passed the two men, their silhouettes faded by the early evening shadows.

Her father kept that smile all the way home – a smile planted from fear, unable to fade because of the terror attached to it. It was not a screaming terror or an obvious incident. That would have been easier for her to bear, like the black writing on the walls saying, "Zionist go home!" or the loud teenaged students yelping, "Jews are worms!' as they had done decades earlier.

This was a sophisticated terror. A silent terror.

When they passed those two men, the quiet outside Mr. Hakim's *hohsh* hit her, and she could feel that there was something very wrong just from the quiet – because of the quiet. The quiet magnified her fears, as she didn't know what to think or expect next in her uncertain world.

When they were down the block from her own *hohsh*, she wondered if she would ever know what happened to Mr. Hakim that day. Maybe she did not want to know.

15

A sleeper had given Mr. Hakim away, tracking him for over a year in an attempt to get his hands on the safe routes out of Syria; actually for the *Mukhabarat* to get their hands on the safe routes. At least that was what Sophia understood later through scattered whisperings in her home. Her father had found this out from those Arab men in the olive oil and perfume shops on the day Hakim had disappeared from his store.

Rose Zalta stood straight, eyeing the wall in front of her with a bucket of soapy water in hand. Sophia spotted the bucket, expecting the usual cleaning project used to shake out her mother's taut nerves. Rose inched behind the sofa and slopped a wet rag on the white wall, thrusting it in every direction.

"They have the wrong man!" Shlomo smacked his forehead with the palm of his hand. "The *Mukhabarat* must have given an agent of theirs a small amount of money to invest with Mr. Hakim in a business venture," he explained. "This way, the agent would be able to track Hakim's pharmaceutical shipments and deliveries to see if they were connected to the safe routes. When Hakim's dealings came up clean, his "business partner" from the *Mukhabarat* decided to try a new strategy to trip Hakim up. He offered to introduce Mr. Hakim to his friend, a supposed smuggler who could help him leave the country. They set him up!"

Rose shook her head. "Why would they do that?" she asked.

"It's hard to tell. Maybe Hakim gave the impression that he would leave if the opportunity arose, and this is their way of dealing with that. I think they were trying to make an example of him regardless, to keep all of us on our toes, to make sure we never forget that they are still strongly on the lookout for this man with the routes."

Sophia's heart skipped a beat. "I heard about this man they have been looking for."

Shlomo turned around with a curious glance. "You have? From where?"

Sophia curled into her chair. "Eva."

Rose lifted her head from the rag. "What about your work, Shlomo? You were doing so well."

"Hashem will help."

Jack rubbed his sweaty palms together. "You can't trust anyone these days! I say it is time we took back our freedom! There are other people nearby who feel the same." Jack's eyes darted to the right and left. "Believe me."

Her mother jumped up. "Shhh! The walls have ears. Lower your voice."

Boomeh came out of the hall with a bundle in her arms. "I think Huda put my linens up here. I left them hanging outside. Jack, your socks are inside-out," Boomeh said to him softly.

"I like them inside-out," Jack said. "They are more comfortable that way."

"I'm going to tidy up downstairs and maybe take a nap," Boomeh said, before letting herself out.

Shlomo sipped his *araq*.

Jack leaned in closer. "What do you think, Garndpa?"

Grandpa Yosef looked up from his *sefer*. "Above all, it is their mission to instill fear in every Jew who tries to escape. They are not so interested in acquiring the safe routes as much as they are in notifying the Jews of what can happen if they dare defy them. The *Mukhabarat* has been known to disguise themselves as Bedouins or Armenians promising safety to Lebanon or Turkey. An innocent youth pays the unknown man up front and follows him trustingly. Days later, they contact the family and bring them in with a cruel interrogation process about the "escape," just to clarify their position to the Jewish community, as a constant reminder that we can't get around them. The youth, though … Let's just say he's lucky if they return him alive."

They sat silently, accepting the truth of Grandpa Yosef's words. Sophia sat back on her heels, seeing her life and the danger they lived with each day. Even Rose Zalta took a break from her scrubbing.

"How do we know if the man with the safe routes

even exists?" Sophia asked. "Has the *Mukhabarat* seen any proof? Or are they just looking for an imaginary person?"

"Does anyone know who he is?" Jack asked.

"No one knows for certain," Sophia's father answered. "This person has been around for a while, though – supposedly for decades now. Gazeem thinks he's probably an importer frustrated with the theft on the main roads. Alternate routes were always sought out by the seasoned businessmen."

Sophia set a glass of water before her father. "Half of the Jewish quarter consists of businessmen. What will they succeed in doing, even if they do find this man?"

"They figure that if they find the real culprit, they will find everything: the routes, the smugglers, their victory. Most of all, like Grandpa said; they will find their opportunity to teach us a lesson."

Rose Zalta pointed a wet rag at her husband. "I have heard quite enough of that. Boomeh is due soon. I think we can all afford to focus on something else right now."

"More scrubbing?" Sophia mumbled.

"What?" her mother asked.

"Nothing." Sophia tried to focus her mind on the baby she'd held in her arms just days before, when she had been assisting her mother. But all she could see was jeopardy stalking the gift of life and waiting for just the right moment to snatch it, mock it, consume it.

"They could be anywhere, these sleepers?" Jack continued to ask.

"No one is safe anymore," Shlomo said.

"We never have been safe," Grandpa Yosef said.

"Safety is just an illusion of Hashem's mercy. We must pray for it at all times."

No one told Boomeh of the bad news. It was everyone's job to keep her comfortable and calm. She slept most of the day anyway during these last months of her pregnancy. Jack dismissed the thought of midwifery and insisted on taking Boomeh to the local hospital whenever the big day arrived. "We aren't taking any chances with this one," he said. "It is important to be professional about this."

Boomeh hadn't said a word to defend midwifery. She had not been able to stop vomiting during the first time she had assisted her mother with a birth, which was also the last time. Rose said nothing either. Jack surprised them all when he assumed a position of authority. Sophia wondered where he had picked up the word "professional".

Boomeh's big day came in late spring. The hospital was so "professional" that they wouldn't let more than one person into Boomeh's room besides hospital personnel. Jack nominated himself as that person, but didn't do much except trip over the machinery and get Boomeh nervous. The doctor was so "professional" that he decided to have Boomeh wait with an inexperienced nurse until it was absolutely necessary for him to come. Jack questioned the nurse over and over again about every detail of everything that was happening. Most of the time, the nurse had to leave Boomeh alone with Jack while she asked her supervisor for the answers. Rose did get to see her daughter for the few moments when Jack decided to take a break. When Shlomo caught on to the whole situation, he grabbed Jack by the shirt and told him to let the women handle Boomeh until the doctor arrived.

Shlomo took Sophia home to get Boomeh's apartment ready. She dusted lightly and washed the sheets while Shlomo did some of the food shopping. The cradle remained in the cellar. No one was to bring it up until the baby was born. No one was to tamper with anything that might bring an *ayin hara* on the baby.

It was Hashem's will for complications to arise, regardless. When Sophia returned later, the doctor arrived and ordered drugs to be administered for the birth. "This is hospital routine, madam," he told Rose. He barked an order at the preoccupied nurse on call. Sophia's mother was the first to notice Boomeh's condition as she showed a negative reaction to the prescribed drug.

"Why is her blood pressure dropping?" the doctor asked. "Nurse!"

A nurse rushed by Sophia, who was standing in the corridor, and ran into Boomeh's room. "I don't know," said the nurse. "It was fine before."

"What is going on?" Rose asked, as the machines sounded and Boomeh began to doze into unconsciousness. "Have you given her anything?"

"We gave her Nubain, which we use for all of our patients. It helps considerably with the birth. Your daughter may be experiencing a negative reaction to it. Anything is possible. Only time will tell."

"What about the baby?" Rose asked.

"If your daughter doesn't snap out of this soon, we may have to speed up this delivery."

Rose lifted Boomeh's frail hand. Boomeh's pulse slowed down until each breath resembled a light quiver.

"We are handling it as best as we can, madam," the doctor repeated in a calm tone. "We go through these kinds of situations every day. Maybe it would be wise for you to wait outside now and let us take care of things. We will keep you updated."

Rose rushed into the hallway and began explaining the situation to Jack.

"What do you mean, 'complications'?"

"Like I said, Jack, there is not much time. Go home and get Abba. Tell him we are still at this hospital on the fifth fl—"

Jack did not hear the last of her instructions. He closed his eyes and fainted in the middle of the hospital floor like a lifeless doll. Rose swerved around to Sophia with Jack's head cupped in her hand. "Go get your father and tell him what's happening. Tell him we need him here! Then go to Aunt Rebecca. Tell her that Boomeh is giving birth. I'll handle Jack."

Sophia ran past Bab Touma and the street of the Roman Arch, all the way home. *If only we had a telephone!* she thought to herself. No phones adorned the walls of Jewish homes. Maybe she should have asked the nurse if she could phone their Palestinian neighbor who lived down the block from their *hohsh*. He could have gotten through to her father sooner. But no, it probably would have taken just as long to get the Palestinian's phone number, and although he did respect Grandpa Yosef, what were the chances of him agreeing to give her father the important message?

Sophia continued running, her clothes becoming absorbed with perspiration and her tumultuous thoughts turned fast into worry. Her high cheekbones swelled and burned in the sun's strong heat. Finally, she reached home, her damp hair clinging to her forehead and hanging limply over her shoulders.

Shlomo answered the door. Sophia breathed in deeply, trying to catch her breath. "I don't know much. Boomeh's condition worsened and Mother wants you to come." She swallowed with no relief, her dry tongue still sticking to the roof of her mouth.

Sophia's father grabbed his jacket and his hat.

"Father, I'm going to tell Aunt Rebecca now."

"No! You stay here. I'll stop by her on my way. Goodbye."

The Palestinian neighbor did come in handy. He drove Shlomo to Aunt Rebecca and then took them both to the hospital, which saved them some twenty minutes of finding a taxicab or taking a long-routed bus ride.

Sophia stayed with her grandfather. She silently served Grandpa Yosef his Turkish coffee with a handful of ka'ak.

Grandpa Yosef patted the dripping saucer with a cloth. "Hashem has His plan, Sophia."

"I know," she said, pulling the Persian rugs out the front door. Grandpa Yosef made an attempt to help her.

"I can do it, Grandpa." She yanked the rugs out the front door. "I may as well get something done."

For the next three hours, Sophia cleaned Boomeh's rooms, washed the rugs in the house, hung them to dry, hurled buckets of water at the walls, and mopped the concrete floors. The bottom of Grandpa Yosef's pants dripped with water. He sat with her the entire time, uninterrupted, rubbing tarnish off the silver Kiddush cup and saucer Sophia had pulled down from the niches in the wall.

Comfort and peace swept through her emotions. Grandpa Yosef seemed to feel that way always. She observed him constantly. Each day was the same, no matter what went on. He bowed his head as the fear of Heaven came upon him, and his heart filled with Hashem's love in return.

Sophia noticed that there was no need for him to raise his voice or even to get frustrated or angry. He didn't expect anything from anyone; therefore, he was never disappointed. When people needed him, though, in his eyes they deserved the utmost respect. In this way, he went in Hashem's ways always.

Sophia used to attribute all this to his age, thinking that he didn't make demands or disrespect people because he was older and had lost most of his steam. Then she realized that Grandpa Yosef's special ways were, in fact, acquired, the results of his constant toiling in Torah and *mitzvot* and continuous polishing of his noble character.

Noise echoed from the courtyard. Sophia spun around and ran to the window. It was her mother, dragging her weary body back from the hospital.

16

"Everything is all right. Thank G-d. The baby, Boomeh, Ja-"

"The baby? The baby!" Sophia jarred her mother. "What is it?"

Rose smiled. "It's a boy and Boomeh is fine."

"*Baruch* Hashem," Grandpa Yosef said.

Rose looked around. "This place is really clean. Where are the rugs?"

"I cleaned them. They are drying outside. Grandpa shined the silver."

Rose let out a sigh. "I almost don't know what to say. Thank you."

"Where is Jack?" Sophia asked.

Shlomo walked in, peeling off his jacket. "They wanted to keep him in the hospital overnight for testing, just in case. He lost consciousness when he fell down on his head."

Rose yanked off her shoes. "The poor boy. He was out longer than Boomeh. The smelling salts were not enough to bring him to. But he seems to be up and stable now."

"What a headache that was," Shlomo said, wiping the sweat off his forehead with a handkerchief.

"What about Boomeh? She didn't look too good," Sophia said.

"At least I was able to stay with her the entire time," Rose said. "Well, not the entire time. It wasn't until that nice doctor walked in that I was able to stay with her. He wasn't at all uptight like the hospital staff. I honestly don't even know where he came from."

"They told me that he was brought in to consult on another patient in the hospital," Shlomo told Rose. "The nurse said that after Jack fainted, Boomeh's condition looked even worse. She was still unconscious. They brought this doctor in immediately. He is young, but highly reputable. He came recently as a consultant to the hospital." Shlomo took off his *tarboosh* and pushed it up over the lip of the dining room cabinet just below the ceiling. "He is one of those top doctors that they have been trying to add to their administration, but he has refused each position they've offered him. He was even flown in on the royal jet to consult one of the princes in Saudi Arabia."

"You know, he reminded me of that nice doctor who helped my friend Yvette," Rose said. "You remember? When her daughters … Out of nowhere he walked in, like, like ..."

"Like an angel?" Grandpa Yosef said.

"Exactly."

"They told me that he plays the harmonica to his patients," Shlomo added.

Rose clasped her hands together. "Isn't that nice!"

"What was wrong with Boomeh in the first place?" Grandpa Yosef asked.

"She was fine before they gave her that drug," Sophia said.

"I was trying to find out myself," Rose said, scrubbing her hands in the kitchen. "It all started with that nice doctor I told you about. He basically took over from the moment he walked in. He examined the vial on Boomeh's tray. I heard him call out, 'Ten-X? Who ordered Ten-X?' Before I knew it, Boomeh was given another drug. He called in a specific dose of Narcon, a medicine to counter the ill effects of the anesthesia they had given her originally."

"Thank G-d it worked," Shlomo said.

"Come to think of it, they did put a new nurse on the job to assist the new doctor. You know, Shlomo, they overdosed on her anesthesia. I'm sure they did, and I'm sure it was that nurse who gave the incorrect dosage. Why else would they have replaced her when this top doctor entered the room? I knew she was no good from the moment we came in."

"Well, it's over now and Boomeh is fine, thank G-d. No need to worry anymore, Rose."

"Especially since we have a *brit milah* to plan," Grandpa Yosef reminded her.

"Hmmm." Sophia's mother stood and walked around in a neat circle. "I think we will make it right here. What do you think?"

"Good idea," Shlomo said. "Your sister Rebecca could use the help right now. Even though it is her responsibility. This is the firstborn child so he will be named after her husband."

"Jack has already told us – about ten times already," Sophia said. "Aharon Ma'alli – not Aharon, not Ma'alli. Only Aharon Ma'alli."

"It will be easier for Boomeh, too. This way, she won't have to go far. We can even have it in the courtyard. Aunt Rebecca should be on her way over now. She said she just had to put together a couple of things."

"It is a good thing that she was spared the details about Jack and his episode," Shlomo said with a grin.

"It's a good thing for Jack," Sophia said.

Shlomo grunted.

"Has anyone seen Huda?" Rose asked. "I haven't seen that black cat of hers either."

Sophia shrugged. "They are probably out together, screaming at each other."

"Sophia, see if you can find her outside," Rose said. "I need her to clean up in Boomeh's apartment. We need to change the linens, dust, and wipe down the walls. I want everything to be spotless for the baby."

"I cleaned the floors, dusted, and changed the sheets," Sophia said.

"That will help, but I still want Boomeh's walls washed. See if you can find our housekeeper."

Down the stairs and around the outdoor room, weeds sprouted from the walls of the servants' quarters. Sophia turned around the corner stone.

"Meow!" the black cat whispered, picking its head up from a small bowl. Dried milk crusted around the bowl's edges.

Sophia stepped back. The cat had been tied to an iron pole with a dirty rag that tugged at its bony ankle when it walked. Sophia touched the pole and shrank back. "Huda?" she called, knocking softly on the door.

The washing board and basin sat upside-down in the corner. A pair of *tzitzit* hung from the clothesline opposite Huda's door, nearly touching the floor. Sophia adjusted the garment, lifting its strings just above the ground. Quiet fell upon her and the scrawny cat. She moved toward the window. Old sheets hung from inside, blocking her view and darkening the little opening she did find where the sheet escaped the window frame.

Sophia picked an orange peel from the windowsill and knelt beside the cat. The cat began to eagerly nibble at it. "If you're so important to her that she has to tie you up, why doesn't she just take you inside with her? Come, cat," Sophia said softly, pulling on the rag to untie it.

"Chashhh!" The cat gnashed its teeth.

"Huda!" Sophia said louder, stepping backward with her eye on the cat. "Huda?" Then Sophia sprang into the courtyard, around the bushes, past the staircase and jumped into the air under the carob tree. A branch grazed her hand. She jumped again, this time with a few slivers of carob in her palm.

"Sophia Zalta!" her mother's voice bellowed from behind.

Sophia wheeled around.

"Did you find her, Sophia?"

"Oh, no, Mother. I knocked. I called outside Huda's door. No one answered."

"We were gone all night and day. I can't imagine where she would be. She never seems to be around when I need her."

"Won't Boomeh be staying in the hospital for a few more days?" Sophia asked, gnawing on the edge of a piece of carob.

"Yes, but Jack will not. It's easier to get things done when he's not here. You know how he is with his privacy and Huda."

"I'll start with the walls if you want. I don't think Huda will be away for long anyway. Her friend, the cat, is tied to a pole outside her door. She wouldn't do that for too long, would she?"

"She tied up the cat?!" Rose grabbed the railing and held onto her skirts, attempting to make the first step.

"It's creepy," Sophia said. "Maybe that is why her cat is always climbing up the fig tree."

"I can't even look. Honestly, I have had it with her. We must start with someone else – as soon as we get settled with Boomeh, after the *brit milah* and the *pidyon haben*."

17

The rabbi announced the *brit milah* to everyone in the *bet hakenesset* that week. All were invited to witness the confirmation of the covenant between the Jewish people and G-d. On the day before the *brit*, the *shamosh* rode his bicycle up and down the bumpy streets of Damascus, knocking on the doors of every community member to tell them personally about the *brit*.

Early in the afternoon, Sophia rocked the baby in her arms while Boomeh dressed and her mother and Aunt Rebecca set up the house. For some reason, an awkward feeling always gnawed at Sophia when she thought of her sister Boomeh's marriage to Aunt Rebecca's son Jack. She turned up the radio just to drown out her thoughts of the idea of two sisters marrying off their children to each other. The music broadcasted from Eretz Yisrael distracted her feelings, but the wondering never stopped. Sophia would be next, and who would they have in mind for her to marry? Her uncle?

Rose Zalta stood at the head of the table and flung a tablecloth into the air while holding onto one edge. Aunt Rebecca leaned forward to catch it at the opposite end.

"It's a good thing Sophia cleaned up after the *Zohar* reading last night," Rose said.

"Where is Huda?" Aunt Rebecca asked.

"I don't know," Rose huffed. "She said that her cat needed medical care and left to a friend who she said would treat the cat for free."

"Today of all days?" screeched Aunt Rebecca.

Sophia brushed the baby's soft hairs with the tips of her fingers. "Why doesn't she just take care of the cat instead of beating it up and then taking it to a doctor? And why did she have to tie its leg to a pole?"

"Huda said that the cat was pulling up the vegetables."

"Because it was hungry, Ma!"

Rose sighed. She flattened out the wrinkles in the tablecloth. "I was hoping your father would speak to her. You know how she doesn't like disappointing him."

"Where is Father? I haven't seen him in three days."

"The courtyard will be much too hot by the time the *brit* begins. We'll have to set up inside," Sophia's mother said, ignoring her daughter's question.

"Less bugs. Good thinking, Rose," Aunt Rebecca said. "I just hope that son of mine comes home in time for the *brit*. He can lose his head sometimes, especially now. He just can't get over the fact that he is a father, you know, that he has a son."

Sophia looked at her mother, still awaiting a response. "Ma?"

Rose lifted her head.

"Father?"

"He's in the oil field."

Aunt Rebecca looked surprisingly at her sister.

"Oil field? For what?" Sophia asked.

"Your father has found new work. Some foreign firm has acquired a permit to explore for oil in the north. Yesterday was his first day." Rose took in a deep breath and hardly released it.

Sophia pulled the blanket over the baby's toes. Her eyes narrowed on her mother. "Oil in the north? Jews are not allowed to travel north. They can't even step out of Damascus without a written permit."

Rose Zalta turned serious. "Your father is doing what it takes to raise his family."

"What does that mean, Ma? Is he in danger?"

"I don't know what paperwork he was able to get. He explained that it was an opportunity he could not miss."

"He *is* in danger," Sophia mumbled. "At least in America, there are tons of job opportunities – safe opportunities."

No one answered and Sophia wondered whether or not they heard, but it didn't matter. She opened a *sefer* Tehillim and began reading while the baby fell asleep in her arms. *Father pumping oil? Probably dressed like an Arab. Hashem, please keep him safe.* Sophia stroked the silky hairline above the baby's cheekbone, whispering the words of Tehillim in a soft rhythm. The baby's fair features relaxed again and she could feel him falling into a deep sleep.

"Miss Rose!" Huda screamed.

The baby's hands fluttered from Huda's voice.

Sophia looked up, startled.

"Huda! You're here."

"Boomeh's party I would not want to miss."

"Good. Please bring in the rest of the chairs so that we can finish setting up inside."

Huda came up the steps a minute later. "I can't bring in the chairs," Huda huffed, chewing on a thread of canvas. "Sand is blowing all over the place. I'm not going out there."

"I'll do it," Sophia said, handing the baby to Aunt Rebecca.

"But your hair!" Rose tried to stop her.

"I'll wash it," Sophia said before pushing open the screen door.

"Now?"

Sophia was already out.

Huda held the door open and watched her speed down the steps. "Let the child help. It is good for her." Huda fluffed her black *chador*.

"Why does Huda have to speak so loudly?" Aunt Rebecca said to her sister, through clenched teeth.

Sophia lifted all of the chairs up the steps. Rose rushed back into the kitchen. "You can help me in here, Huda. Oh, and Huda, the baby is sleeping."

"The more noise he gets used to, the better he'll be," Huda said, pointing her arm in the air. "I was raised in my father's blacksmith shop. All that banging did me good. I don't care for quiet and I don't want it."

"Will someone tell her to be quiet? We have work to do." Aunt Rebecca wove out of the stacked chairs. "Let me help, Sophia. You can't do everything yourself. It gets tiring. Just like your mother, taking care of everything herself."

She eyed the display of the set table and nodded approvingly. "That looks nice. I still wish you'd let me help with the preparing, Rose."

"I'm too nervous anyway," Rose said. She looked up at the clock on the wall. "Shlomo. I hope he makes it."

Sophia stepped into her parents' room. She softly opened the desk drawer and sifted through a tattered *sefer*, papers, a few pencils, and some loose coins. Her hand reached to the back of the drawer until she felt the card and pulled it out. *He did not bring it for a reason. If caught, it would mean his death.* She uncurled the edges of her father's identity card. The bold red letters of the word "*Musawi*" spread across the top. She dropped the card back into the drawer and slammed it shut, silencing the harrowing reminder of their decreed lives.

"Did I tell you, Rose, that I invited that nice doctor?" Aunt Rebecca said.

"The one from the hospital? I'm glad you did. He's the same one who helped Yvette, you know, when I went to see her. Such a fine young man."

Sophia's aunt cooed over the baby, while Boomeh lit up and smiled at each comment. Sophia barely flinched when Boomeh said, "Look, Ma!" and both her mother and aunt looked up. It didn't matter anymore.

Then Sophia's thoughts got the better of her. What

else had worn away at her? What else could her mind be conditioned to accept just because her sister did it? *Everything and nothing,* Sophia decided. Everything, if she adapted to someone else's life just because she was having trouble acquiring her own, and nothing, if she could see her own self in each step of her life, even if she wasn't in control of it. Living her life through her own eyes would be her only chance at happiness and peace of mind, even if she did marry her first cousin and spent the rest of her life in Syria.

She folded the napkins, defining their creases and placement. She kept folding, creasing, and firmly placing the napkins – creasing and pressing, creasing and pressing, until her aunt touched her arm and said, "I don't think you can iron them any better than that."

✶　✶　✶

The heat of the day peaked at mid-afternoon. Her mother nudged the tray of Eliyahu Hanavi into Sophia's hands as soon as the *mohel* walked in. Sophia tried to balance the three-tiered platter while standing patiently for guests to light a candle and toss some coins on the tray. It was a *segulah* for all who participated in the custom, especially for the person holding the tray. The honor was mostly given to single girls next in line for a bright future, and since Sophia no longer went to school, her purpose for holding the tray seemed all the more practical.

The prayers began and the tray filled with light down to the last candle. Sophia inched toward the window, hoping to sneak a peek at her father making it in time for the *brit milah*. The prayers escalated and then a booming voice entered the room, followed by cheering. Shlomo Zalta walked straight up to the group of men who had begun the prayers, taking his place beside Jack.

Sophia smiled as she looked on at her father.

Jack motioned to the chair beside him, giving over the honor of *sandek* to Sophia's father, as Jack's father had insisted. Sophia watched the look on her father's face as his tired body sank into the chair. The look of joy almost covered the sadness she had been seeing in him more and more as the days passed. She turned away, ashamed to discover vulnerability in her father.

"Sophia? Guess who!"

Sophia twisted around, the grip of her friend barely covering her eyes. "Eva! You are late! I had to hold this tray all by myself."

"I brought some friends. Our teacher let us out early today."

Sophia gave a small wave to the couple of girls behind Eva. "Thank you for coming."

The crowd quieted as soon as Aunt Rebecca entered the room with the baby. The baby wore a white knitted *kippah* that was tied under his chin and a shiny white robe. Aunt Rebecca's right shoulder rose above her left as she struggled to keep the baby firmly in place on the slippery satin pillow. It offered no traction and her expression seemed to tangle with each step forward. Several people patted the satin pillow as Aunt Rebecca walked by, hoping it would bring them good *mazal*. One older woman patted the baby and held onto his robe just a few seconds too long. As a horrified Sophia looked on from afar, unable to do anything about it from where she stood, the baby slid halfway off the pillow as Aunt Rebecca entered the crowd.

"The baby!" Sophia screeched.

Gasps rose from the crowd and Sophia's heart sank, thinking that her call had come too late. The baby fell down and a wave of people bent over to see where the baby had gone.

"Oh, please, Hashem, let him be alright! Please!" Sophia stretched up on her toes to see better what had happened.

"Was that the baby?" Eva put her arm on Sophia's shoulder.

One of Eva's friends panted, "Oh, no! The baby! The baby! Is the baby, is the baby—"

Shlomo Zalta stood with the baby in his arms, lifting him a bit for the crowd to see. "He's fine." Then he shook hands with the man beside him and the rest of the group took turns slapping the man on the back and pointing toward him.

"He saved the baby. That man saved the baby!" Eva said.

"Yes, it was him!" called her friend.

Sophia's eyes shifted around. "Who?" she whispered to Eva.

"You can't see him now," Eva said. "His back is turned to us. He is the tall one standing one in front and two to the left of your father. Wait … he just moved. Two to the front and two to the left of your father." Sophia smiled at the way Eva could identify anyone without having to move a finger.

"He's new in town."

Sophia elbowed her friend and made a mental note that the man who saved the baby was wearing a blue suit jacket and a white shirt.

Jack raised his voice in song and the crowd responded at the start of the ceremony. When the *mohel* finally finished, Rose Zalta entered the crowd to bring the baby – little Aharon Ma'alli – back to Boomeh, while the rest of the crowd lingered near Sophia's father to get a *berachah* from the *sandek*.

Most of the guests were still talking about the man in the blue suit jacket who saved the baby. Finally, he turned around and Sophia was able to identify him – his unmistakable grin, his arresting eyes seizing a view of the festivities. Shock snatched her heart. Her knees weakened and her legs seemed to sink straight into her feet. She held onto Eva's shoulder for support. A tremor crawled through her body as the sounds of the gunshots outside the Armenian wedding revisited her.

"What are you looking at, Sophia Zalta?" Eva shook her head mockingly from side to side.

"The Arab guest," Sophia mouthed, but more words did not follow.

"What?" Eva asked. "You look like you've seen a demon. Is everything okay?"

"Yes. Fine." Sophia turned toward the door. "I need some air." She pushed the door open. *Why would anyone invite that Arab to the* brit milah? she thought. *What was he doing here?* She would have to ask her mother or Aunt Rebecca.

She looked up across the courtyard, remembering how she had burst through the *hohsh* door after escaping the gunshots of the Arab boy. She looked behind her, her stomach churning as she envisioned the snorting boy with the gun just before the Arab guest jumped on him. A clear image repeated itself. *"Run!"* the Arab guest had yelled her way. Why did he do that? She had saved herself, running around the cart, cutting her leg, and dashing down the street, or maybe it was the Arab guest who had saved her?

A soft whining broke into her thoughts outside. A small branch from the carob tree fell onto its trunk, its leaves shaking in the sunlight. "Oh, no, not again." Sophia ran down the stairs and sped to the tree. Above her head, Huda's cat screeched as its paws slipped down the bark. "Are you stuck up in that tree again? Sit on the branch, cat," Sophia called up the tree. "Can you reach it?" She took in a deep breath. "You'll probably fall first."

Sophia looked down at her ivory chiffon dress that her mother had bought for her special for Boomeh's engagement party just a year ago. It would be too late to change. She ran to the cellar door where she had left Gazeem's old gardening boots. There, she kicked off her shoes and yanked on the boots. Without tying the laces, she raced back to the tree, the boot laces flapping in every direction.

Anchoring herself on the sturdier branches, Sophia skillfully climbed the tree. When she pulled herself up, hand over hand, a wave of recognition overcame her. She remembered the same sense of accomplishment she used to feel each time she climbed the tree – an accomplishment judged by her alone.

"Look at you!" she said to the cat. "How did you get up here?" The cat practically jumped into her arms. "I have you," Sophia comforted it. "Just hold on tight now."

As they made their way down, a sharp twig caught the side of her dress. One hand held onto the branch above and her other hand held tightly to the cat. Only midway down, it was still too high up to let go of the cat. Sophia twisted, trying to free herself, and tore her dress in the process. Finally, she cleared the branches and bent her knees to jump down. She tried to release the cat from her grip, but it seemed too afraid, even from that height. "Here we go," she said before jumping with the cat in her arms. She landed flat on the soles of the gardening boots, unaware of the pair of eyes that had been watching her heroism from the start.

"If you wanted to play, cat, you just had to say so," she said, stroking him. She looked up at the front door, wondering if the Arab guest had left yet. "Come, let's put some water in that dish of yours." Then Sophia disappeared into the courtyard, carrying the cat behind the wall of the servants' quarters.

18

Her heart was a pool of fearful conclusions.

"There is no use waiting forever for you to marry. How patient am I expected to be?" asked her father. "I saw a nice boy. He asked about you, so I jumped at the opportunity. What exactly *are* you waiting for, young lady?"

Sophia dropped the sack of rice she had carried up from the cellar and looked over at her mother.

"It's not like he's just any boy from the street, Sophia. He's a doctor," her mother said.

"He is extremely gifted. The head sheik of Saudi Arabia is determined to appoint him as royal physician. His name is Matlub Laniado. He spotted you at the *milah*," her father said. "You must have made a good impression."

"Impression? I didn't even speak to him. Are you sure he means me?"

Shlomo laughed heartily.

For Sophia, the room turned into a dark forest at her father's amusement, where traps and snares lay at each turn in the road. She was target practice for any hunter and there was no place to hide.

"Shlomo," Rose said, eyeing her husband, "tell her that he is the one who saved Boomeh in the hospital, and also the one who saved the baby at the *brit milah*."

Sophia stifled a gasp. Her thoughts racing, she picked at the small hole in the trim of the tablecloth until it widened and tore at the seam. "I've seen him before, this doctor who saved the baby. He can't be Jewish."

Her mother pulled the cloth out of Sophia's reach. "What do you mean? The Laniados have lived in Halab for centuries. They are fine Jews."

"He can't be Jewish, Mother. He's an Arab." She turned plainly to her mother. "You have set me up with an Arab?"

"What are you talking about? No one said he was an Arab!" Shlomo hollered.

Her head pounded louder. "Remember that drunken boy I told you about from the Armenian wedding, the one who almost shot me to death?"

"When you cut your leg?"

"Yes. *He* was with him. This doctor," Sophia said. "He had a mustache at the time. He was grinning ... laughing ... or maybe ..." She suddenly stopped. "I don't know!"

"You must be mistaken," her father said. "He could be reminding you of that person you did see. Our minds can do that to us."

The deep associations that accompanied her fears always surpassed those that accompanied her joys. "I am certain it is him," Sophia said. "I can still hear the gunshots."

"It is possible that he did go to that wedding as a Jewish associate or business partner of those Armenians. It is not uncommon," her father said.

"Shlomo, maybe we should have asked her first," Rose interrupted.

Sophia's father banged his fist on the end table beside him. "I am exercising my right as her father – just as my father did before me. No more discussions!"

Rose stood up at her husband's crisp response. "You have something nice to wear, I'm sure," she said. "Come, let's go inside. I will help you."

Sophia opened her mouth to speak, but she never did express her pain – the inability to discuss her dream of leaving Damascus.

"He'll be here at the end of the week, young lady. You have plenty of time to get yourself ready."

"And I will try to be home," Rose said.

"Where are you going?" Sophia asked.

"I have several births expected this week." Sophia's mother looked up at the clock. "I promised I would be there."

"Rose, I probably won't be here. I am leaving for the north this afternoon," Shlomo said.

"Again?" Rose's voice rose an octave. "Are you certain it is safe?"

"I'll be fine."

"And who will be here to receive our Arab guest?"

Sophia asked, waiting for her father's reaction.

Shlomo Zalta threw his daughter a sideways glance.

"I should be here; don't worry. Let's see what you'll be wearing." Rose headed for Sophia's room. "Maybe we should ask Jack to be around, just in case."

"Jack?" Sophia asked. "Boomeh's Jack?"

Shlomo smiled at the horrified look on his daughter's face. "Hashem has a way of making things work out, Sophia. Try to enjoy yourself."

The night of her meeting, as soon as the evening broke into the day's heat, Sophia took a walk in the courtyard. After taking only a few steps, she suddenly caught sight of a familiar-looking handle sticking out from behind the wall of the cellar. *The cart?* She cautiously lunged at the handle, then darted behind the wall. Sure enough, there stood her old cart, the last bottles of *araq* still lying on their bellies inside of it.

She looked around the courtyard. She had left it outside the Armenian *hohsh* just before she had escaped. Almost a year had passed since then. Who had brought it back?

The bottles felt smooth under her fingertips when she rubbed them. Her hands trembled as she held onto the handle of the cart. She bent down, running her palm over the wood to see where it had cut into her leg. It felt as smooth as the wooden table in her house. She felt the other side – just as smooth. She stepped back, trying to judge if this was, in fact, her cart.

"Sophia!" Boomeh called out from the house, waving from the window. "Aren't you ready yet? He'll be here soon."

Sophia moaned. It was just a matter of time until the minutes ate up her solitude completely and she would have to face him. She walked toward the house, her eyes still on the cart – on its smooth edges, on the bottles inside, on the mystery of who had returned it after all this time.

Maybe it's my wedding present from the Arab guest, she thought sarcastically. She turned her eyes to Heaven. "Hashem," she pleaded, "if he is my *naseeb*, please let me see it. Let it be clear to me who he really is."

She hurried up the stairs where Boomeh held the door halfway open.

Jack sat on the sofa with the baby. Huda stood at the sink, piling up the clean dishes. "What about my raise?" Huda repeated.

"Mother will be home soon," Boomeh told her.

"Well, it's either the raise or a hot water tank for the laundry downstairs."

Boomeh ushered Sophia to her room. "You had better hurry up. Jack will do his best to welcome your guest. I'm going to check on Huda."

"Huda, you can use the hot water tank here, in the kitchen," she heard Boomeh say.

"In the kitchen? And carry the clothes up and down the stairs?! That's it! I'm going to sleep."

Sophia closed the door.

White shirts and several skirts hung stiffly in her small closet. She pulled out what her mother had set aside for her – the same outfit she had worn when she had gone out last time, about a year ago. A single thread dangled from the skirt hem. Sophia turned the hem over. The stitching had unraveled. Half of the hem would be down by the end of the night. She twisted her head to see the clock. Only ten minutes left.

What would she do if her father was wrong, if he had set her up with the Arab guest after all?

She came down the hall eight minutes later, wearing a black pleated skirt with a white top, a black belt, single pearl earrings, and her hair curling to the side. "Boomeh," she whispered loudly, her lips red from the drying sun. "Boomeh, are you there? I need a hairclip."

She rushed down the hall. "Boomeh? Jack?" she called, peering into the empty rooms. "Maybe I'll be greeting the Arab guest myself after all!" She swung the door open, hoping to rush to Boomeh's apartment before he arrived.

Shock interrupted her stride at the sight of the young man standing before her, his fist clenched mid-air, in position to knock on the door. He stood a head above her, tall and dark, with deep-set eyes, definitely the same person who had saved the baby, but was he the Arab guest?

19

Matlub smelled of the flowers in Damascus that bloomed on April nights and the steady desert breezes swept inland to relieve the city's inhabitants of the oppressive heat.

"Going somewhere?" he asked her.

Sophia's nerves released a light laugh. "Hi. Please come in," she said.

Rose Zalta rushed to the door at the sound of it opening. "Oh, Sophia, there you are. And you must be Matlub, yes? I recognize you from the hospital. Such a *malach* you were, coming in at just the right time for Boomeh, and then for Boomeh's baby. I heard you rescued the baby, I mean, caught him just before he … you know, at the *milah*, they all told me."

Matlub lowered his head. "Pleasure to meet you," he said.

"Come in. Sit down a moment," Rose said, motioning to the armchair beside the coffee table dressed with dried apricots, dates, pistachio nuts, and china bowls. "My husband regrets that he is unable to greet you personally. He is away for a few days."

Sophia flattened her hair behind her ear. "You finished up with the birth?" she asked her mother.

"Just barely," her mother said. "Where is Jack?"

"Don't know." She sat on the sofa beside her mother, who sat across from Matlub. *Maybe he isn't the Arab guest*, she thought, eyeing his polite manner.

Sophia reached for the black hairpin that she had left behind the lamp on the end table and slipped it into her hair.

Rose rubbed out the wrinkles in her skirt when she sat. "So how is your family? Still in Halab I hear."

"Just my parents and my sisters." A purity softened his dark, refined features when he spoke. He crossed his legs at the ankles and cupped his hands in his lap.

Sophia fingered the pin in her hair that held her curls in a soft design. Her thumb paced over the top of the pin, feverishly tracing the ridges that rolled evenly in ripples. Was he the Arab guest from the Armenian wedding or wasn't he?

"And your brother? Don't you have a younger brother?"

"Yes, I do," was all he said.

Rose nodded silently. Just by the absence of his words, Sophia knew that his brother had escaped.

The front door swung open. Jack peered into the room, holding a bottle of *araq* in his hand.

Rose beckoned to him. "Come in, Jack."

"Oh, boy," Sophia mumbled.

"I came as quick as I could to meet our honored guest." Jack strode over to Matlub and extended his free hand to him, giving Matlub a hearty handshake. "I had to put my son to sleep, but I was looking out for you from the window. You must have just snuck in." He gave Matlub a light punch on the shoulder.

Sophia shifted in her seat, watching Jack hang himself on every facet of his unpredictable behavior.

Jack raised the bottle of *araq* in the air. "This calls for a celebration!"

Sophia closed her eyes tightly.

Jack wrestled with the cork and nodded at Sophia. "Some glasses, young lady." She hesitated for a minute, flinching at his usage of the term by which only her father called her.

"Oh, don't trouble yourself for me," Matlub said. "I save my *araq* for Shabbat."

"Don't be silly," Jack insisted, his face as twisted as his grip on the bottle.

"Honestly, Jack," Rose interrupted, "I'm certain that Matlub has plans of his own."

Matlub stood up and looked over at Sophia. "Whenever you are ready."

She stood at the confidence in his tone.

The cart remained to the left of the *hohsh* door. As soon as the two of them had left, Matlub crossed behind her and grabbed a brown paper bag from inside it.

Sophia stared at the bag and then at him.

"I didn't want to bring it inside. It's a surprise for you."

Sophia smiled, happy for the dark night that masked her emotions.

On the street, he turned to her. "So how is your leg?"

Sophia looked down at her legs. "Leg? What do you mean?" she asked, smiling dreadfully.

They had already turned the corner at the end of Sophia's street. "Didn't you cut your leg on the cart? I noticed the blood on the protruding wood before I shaved it down."

His words. They rang through her ears. Fear numbed her and slowed her footsteps to a halt while panic filled every space within her.

He stopped beside her. "Did I say something wrong?"

"So it was you who returned the cart?"

"After the wedding that night, I kept it. I didn't know who you were until I saw you at the *milah*." His arresting eyes and unmistakable grin testified for his words. He was the Arab guest.

"Who are you?" she asked, her eyes narrowed.

"Officially, I am Matlub Laniado."

"Officially?" she asked, beginning to walk slowly in the direction they were going.

"My name is Matlub Laniado. I am twenty-three years old. I was born in Halab to Shlomo and Adele Laniado. I am currently doing some work at the hospital in Damascus City. I used to dream of becoming a pilot, my favorite food is *kibbe*, and I enjoy cooking."

"I didn't mean for you to …" she started.

"Alright, let's start over. Hi, I'm Matlub."

"What were you doing ... never mind," she said. "Remind me to ask you later about the wedding."

He led her at a quicker pace and she followed.

"The groom of the wedding fainted that day. I was sent there to revive him before they pushed him down the aisle."

"You had a mustache."

"A fake one," he said. "They gave them out at the wedding. All the little boys ran around with them, saying that they were not men until they wore a mustache."

Sophia giggled.

"The boy's father would not let me go until the ceremony was over. I was just leaving as you were walking by." He hardly slowed down; he glanced to the right, he glanced to the left, and yet he never moved his head.

Sophia watched the contents of the bag shift slightly as he hummed a tune. She walked beside him and wondered what was inside. From Sharat Amin, he led her up Tele Hill.

"Isn't this the way to ..." Her heart skipped a beat, terrified to even utter the word. The official headquarters of the *Mukhabarat* sat dimly to their right. A woman in a *chador* stepped out of the building. From her walk, she could have been Huda.

Two men dressed in plainclothes drooped against the entrance while they puffed on their cigarettes. One of the men threw his cigarette to the ground, the oversized mole on his cheek visible from the light of the few occupied spaces inside the building.

Sophia shuddered.

"Don't worry," he said softly. "Our destination is up ahead."

Sophia advanced with rigid steps, afraid to lift her head – afraid to incriminate herself for something she did not even do. The basement of that building filled her thoughts. The *Mukhabarat* was known for its creative tortures conducted down there, reserved especially for those unfortunate enough to stay as overnight guests.

They walked downhill and stopped in the middle of an orchard overlooked by the *Mukhabarat*. From above, the tops of their heads blended into the orchard-like tree stumps. Matlub opened the bag and pulled out a dark blanket, which he spread to the left of a tall fence. Leaves filled the fence, dividing the orange trees from their neighboring crop. There, the two of them escaped the view of the *Mukhabarat* and enjoyed a view of their own, surveying red rooftops below and a clear night sky above.

"Have a seat," Matlub motioned to her. He set the bag down on the soft blanket between them and pulled out two bundles wrapped in white dishtowels, two small jugs of water, two paper cups, and some mandarins. The mandarins scented the placid breeze which blew in from the orange grove below. Matlub offered her a jug to wash her hands. Sophia unwrapped one of the bundles in the light of the moon, exposing an *ejjeh* sandwich on a small plate, a fork, a knife, paper napkins, and the dishtowel on her lap that, she assumed, was supposed to serve as a placemat. She set the contents of the first bundle in front of Matlub, unwrapped the second one for herself, and smiled down at the food on her lap.

"I told you I like to cook," he said, after he washed his own hands and took his first bite.

Only the background music of toads and crickets could be heard, the typical symphony of nighttime creatures at their best. Workmen unloaded a truck twenty meters below. "That is Mr. Cohen," Matlub said, pointing at someone wearing a soft tan cap. He waved, catching the man's attention. "He assured me that we would not be alone tonight. He'll be here until dawn with his brother and the rest of their crew."

Light from the tractor entered the clearing where they sat. "This is really good," Sophia said between bites.

He smirked. "I was trying to make a good impression."

"When we began walking up Tele Hill …" Sophia started to say.

"I know. I saw the look on your face. I hope you are okay with it," he said. "There are few spots where I can come alone to just sit and think. This is one of them. The orchard belongs to Mr. Cohen, whose son is a friend of mine."

"It's nice," she said, watching the leaves from a tree dangle over their heads. "It reminds me of my climbing days as a child."

"Mmmh. But I'm sure that building," he said, pointing his thumb behind him, "puts fear into just about every one of us."

Sophia shuddered at his words. "I had two friends," she said. "They didn't make it."

He looked at her and for the first time, she saw gentleness in his eyes.

"They must have had such dreams," she continued, shivering.

"My brother left," Matlub said. "We still haven't heard from him. It was very difficult for my family … in many ways."

"And you don't share your brother's dream?" She closed her lips tightly as soon as her words escaped.

"He left to start fresh with a life of freedom. I guess that is what everyone wants." He turned to her and smiled. "I am partial to Syrian girls, though, so I stayed put."

Startled, Sophia asked, "Is that why you became a doctor? To plan for security while living in this insecure place?"

"That was my plan, but let's see what our Father in Heaven has planned for us all. Who knows if being a doctor will mean anything in a year or even six months from now?"

Loud voices rose in anger from the bottom of the hill. "There are only ten here," Mr. Cohen said. "I paid for twenty."

"That's all I got!" hollered the Muslim.

Mr. Cohen followed him to the car. "What about my crop?"

"You'll have to talk to my boss."

"I did speak to your boss. He said that he had just loaded twenty cases on the truck for me."

The Muslim ignored Mr. Cohen and pulled away, nearly running over his foot. Mr. Cohen wiped his brow with his handkerchief.

The vexation on Mr. Cohen's face reached them, filling the air around them and painting it with all the tragedy and pain that raised them from infancy as a people severed from the rights of their society.

Sophia tapped on the tree beside her. "Sometimes I wonder if this world is even real," she said, following the sturdy lines up the tree's swerving trunk with her eyes.

"What do you mean?"

"I feel like I'm acting in a play, only I don't know what's in the script or when it will end—" she stopped herself short. "Do you ever feel that way?"

"Yes," he assured her. "I do."

Sophia brushed her hands together, rolling the cool mist off her fingertips, and tucked her hands under her skirt.

"Are you cold?" Matlub asked, fishing through the bottom of the bag he brought. He pulled out a woven wool blanket and dropped it beside her.

"Thank you," she said, draping it over her shoulders. She recalled her dream of escaping Damascus and found that it came to her vividly only when she was in misery. Now, her dream sat wrapped and camouflaged by layers of curiosity about the young man who sat beside her.

"And your dream?" he asked her. "You must have one of your own."

She wrapped the blanket more tightly around her. Within her mind she hunted for the right thing to say, but her fuzzy dream of leaving Damascus sat firmly in her thoughts, taking root and refusing to budge.

Matlub pressed her for a response with his silence until she could not hold it in any longer. "My brothers live in the Aretz," she said. "I've always dreamt of following them."

He rubbed his thumb beneath the even hairs that softly covered his chin.

She pulled up a blade of grass beside her and twisted it around her finger. "I suppose that would be an irresponsible thought on my part."

He looked out into the distance and shook his head slightly. Two small dimples formed on his cheeks. "You've thrown me off, Sophia Zalta."

"I didn't mean to."

"I understand now," he said, nodding his head. "Your heart is set on leaving Syria."

His directness restrained her. Every cell in her face went limp so that she could no longer attempt even the faintest smile.

Matlub gathered the utensils, plates, cups, and orange peels on the cloth and tied it before stuffing it into the brown bag. Then he looked at Sophia. "Most people feel the same way you do. They are just too afraid to say it out loud."

Sophia tossed an extra cup in the bag. The tightness in her face eased a bit. "And what about your dreams?" she asked.

"They are simple: to find a decent person to share my life with."

"And you haven't found her yet?"

He picked up a bunch of loose flowers from the ground, tied them with a stem, and set it down in front of her. "I just started looking, Sophia Zalta."

He stretched his long legs and looked down the hill at Mr. Cohen, who had just about finished setting everything out for the morning.

Sophia picked up the flowers at her side and inhaled the dizzying mixture of their scents. She watched the way Matlub stared at Mr. Cohen a moment longer. The moon lit up his profile, and Sophia could read his pain for Mr. Cohen just by the way his shoulders dropped.

After a while, Matlub spoke up. "Shall we go?" he asked.

They walked through the orchard a little bit more before they headed onto the road. This took them out of their way, but they avoided passing the *Mukhabarat* towering over them.

Sophia wondered whether he had purposely avoided the *Mukhabarat* in order to comfort her. They walked side by side. The loudest sound they heard were their footsteps scraping the old stones beneath them, intruding on the quiet stillness of the night.

"Can I ask you a question?" she asked finally.

He glanced at her. "Anything."

Sophia smiled hesitantly. "When you left the Armenian wedding that night and saw the Arab boy pointing his gun at me, why did you tell him to shoot?"

Matlub hummed his tune again. "What did you think?"

"At first, I thought you were as twisted as he was, maybe even more – commanding him to shoot until his gun was finally empty. I watched you jump on him, but only when I reached home did I realize that you might have done all that just to save me." She looked up at him.

He shifted his bag to his other hand and she could see a reluctant smile spread across his face. "I guess you will never know."

From the next road, they could see outside the Jewish Quarter. Matlub looked casually at the entrance where a military truck was stationed just outside the gates.

Sophia assumed he had lost his sense of direction. "My *hohsh* is ..."

"Yes," he said. His gaze still lingered on the truck.

"What was that truck doing there?" she asked when they were finally at her street.

"I'm not sure."

Outside, a light breeze swept through the fig tree by her house and rustled its leaves. Sophia plucked a single leaf off the branch that dipped down in front of her and rubbed its furry skin. Matlub's eyebrows furrowed as if her action had confirmed some unknown truth to him and he sat on the edge of the cistern. She leaned on the stone rim and peered into the still dark water.

"What are you thinking about?" she asked.

"Just something I witnessed here at the *brit milah*."

She glanced at her *hohsh*. Different events raced through her mind; her setting up the chairs, bringing up the *araq*, holding the baby.

"I saw you climb the tree."

Uneasiness clenched her heart. Gazeem's gardening boots perched against the wall of the staircase as witnesses to her act.

"You saved the cat."

"I-I was just in the right place at the right time."

"I think you are a lot more than that. In your strength, you carry the *middah* of kindness. That's a rare combination."

Sophia cleared her throat, although it didn't need clearing.

Their feet lazily woke up the dust on each step they took up the stairs to her *hohsh*.

She slipped a key out of her pocket and unlocked the door. "Good night," she said, slanting her head to see him. "Dinner was delicious; thank you."

"I'm glad." Matlub pushed his hands deep into his pockets. Then he lifted his stare from the ground. Sincerity filled his eyes. "I would like to see you again, Sophia."

20

A Tehillim reading took place in Sophia's home the next morning. Ten men filled the front room; ten men united in despair; ten men immersed in prayer; ten men determined to bring down mercy from Heaven. The climax of their wailing melody lifted her from her sleep, filling her with an immediate uneasiness.

Shlomo Zalta came in early that morning. Sophia helped her mother serve cake and twisted cheese to the group who had just finished reciting *sefer* Tehillim.

"What can we do?" one of the men asked.

"There is nothing we can do," said another, shaking his head. "Nothing but pray."

"Do you think it was because of that sleeper everyone has been talking about? We can't just let that sleeper make trouble for us and get away with it," Jack said.

Shlomo Zalta spoke up. "It's possible that the rumor

about Assad himself sending one of his generals to shape up the Jewish Quarter is because of that sleeper. The sleeper could have let him know about the recent escape, and it caused too much embarrassment to Assad."

Sophia could almost see the scene from the night before when Matlub stopped at the opening in the street that allowed a view of the mysterious military truck. Was that truck sent from Assad to "shape up the Jewish Quarter," as her father put it?

"Zalta, as you know, talk of the sleeper has been going on for some time now. You yourself have told us that a sleeper has recently surfaced in our neighborhood. I'm sure it's the sleeper who is feeding Assad his information. And that must be why Assad sent the truck." This came from the first man who had initiated the conversation, a big-boned, swarthy fellow.

Comments began to fly among the group. "If we are smart, we can get that sleeper before he causes real damage!"

"Who could it be?"

"Let's go through some possibilities."

"The truck was not discovered until last night, and it was discovered near your street, Zalta," the outspoken, big-boned man said, turning to Sophia's father. "Has anyone unusual been hanging around your street? Anyone new whom you wouldn't trust?"

Sophia gasped. Her father looked up.

"Anyone in the last twenty-four hours?"

She imagined what would happen if her father mentioned Matlub.

Shlomo Zalta pushed back his chair from the table that they were all crowding around. Everyone fell silent, waiting for his response. "I'll be in touch with you if we come up with something," was all he said. He ushered everyone to the front door. "Not to worry. I'll be in touch."

When everyone left, Rose Zalta reached for the chair behind her and slowly fell into it. "What does that mean, Shlomo?"

"I'm not sure," Shlomo said, rubbing the sweat off his forehead. He pointed to Sophia. "You want to talk about last night, young lady?"

"I saw the truck outside the gates, Father. Actually, Matlub noticed it first."

"When was that?"

"On our way home. It was late."

Shlomo Zalta let out a deep breath.

"We haven't done anything ... wrong!" Sophia's last few words ended flat as she realized that Syria's harsh decrees weren't always indicative of their actions.

"That is irrelevant. They will choose the innocent from time to time just to remind us of their capabilities. Besides, they have an agenda. Gazeem says that they are committed to locating the safe routes out of Syria. Everyone knows about the two Jewish boys who escaped this week."

"Hashem should protect them," Rose interrupted.

"How do they know?" Sophia asked.

"The hired Muslim who brought them to Turkey is hanging by his neck in the city square for everyone to see."

Rose took the rag in her hand and scrubbed violently at the scuff mark on the foot of the table.

"Their eyes are open to any clues that will lead them to these routes and the person behind them. Word has it that this Muslim even confirmed the legend of the one behind the maps."

The map she had found and the broken dream that clung to it surfaced in her thoughts. Sophia drew the curtains and popped her head out from between them. "Won't people say just about anything under duress, especially to shift the blame off themselves? How can they be sure that the Muslim was saying the truth?"

Shlomo Zalta stared at his daughter. "I imagine that they are not taking any chances."

Rrrunnk, rrrunnk, rrrunnk, rrunnk! The door rumbled in its metal frame. Jack's voice followed the sound of the pounding. "It's me! Open up. It's Jack."

Jack stepped in and let out an eager sigh. "What are we doing about this truck? It looks abandoned. No one has stepped in or out. It is driving me crazy!"

Shlomo sat down. "There is nothing we can do."

Jack raised his voice. "I have friends. All of us say the same thing. We have had enough of this. Why don't we fight back?"

Shlomo Zalta sighed.

"There are three thousand of us. If we all stick together, we can make a difference!" Jack jutted his head toward the corner of the room. "Grandpa?"

Grandpa Yosef stopped reading from his *sefer*. Jack walked over to him slowly and leaned down.

"Anger has the power to mask all of our senses," Grandpa whispered. He lifted the *sefer*. It trembled in his palms. "Haven't we been through worse than this? Much worse!"

Jack froze in place. Grandpa Yosef patted Jack's cheek lightly.

"Well, we have to do something," Jack protested. "We can't just let them do what they want with us. Now that I have a son, it matters even more."

"I know it does," Grandpa said. "We all want to create a wonderful environment for all of our children. It's important to focus on the whole picture, though, and not get distracted by details."

"What about the truck?"

"The truck is just another detail, one in a string of many that may prove to mean something or prove to mean nothing. We will know in time. Everything surfaces eventually."

"So I'm supposed to just sit here? There must be something we can do!"

"Yes, there is something. Your wife hasn't slept at all last night. That baby of yours has been keeping her up around the clock. Helping her out is your primary duty right now."

Jack grinned sheepishly. He rubbed his face and waved shortly before leaving.

Sophia locked the door behind him.

Shlomo and his wife pulled Sophia to sit down. "And how was your meeting?"

"Nice," Sophia said.

"What did you think of him?"

"He is interesting, nice, and sort of … at peace with himself."

Shlomo raised his eyebrow. "Which means that ..."

"I would go out with him again, Father."

Shlomo smiled and pinched his daughter's chin. "I will be in touch with the matchmaker, with G-d's help."

21

G-d's help can come in many different disguises. Norma the matchmaker met with Sophia and her parents after many attempts on her father's part to get Sophia a second meeting with Matlub.

"He just disappeared!" she said, throwing her hands up in bewilderment. "Believe me, I have my reasons for wanting to contact him. And not just for you. An eligible and handsome boy is not easy to find. Many other girls are waiting in line for him. So when I say he disappeared, believe me, he disappeared. He just got up and vanished."

"Did you hear back from him at all after the first meeting?" Rose asked. "How did he feel about it?"

"I didn't have the chance. The last time I spoke to him was before they went out. Such a fine boy. He asked me if a picnic in the orchard would be appropriate."

Sophia's words cracked in her tone. "He did?"

Sophia's mother shook her head. "This doesn't make any sense."

"Where is the boy now?" Shlomo asked.

"Like I said," Norma repeated in a slow and deliberate tone, "I have no idea where he went. He could have left the country for all I know. I tried to contact his family in Halab. No one knows where he is."

Through the sheer curtains, Huda's hand swiped the window pane from the outside with a rag.

"Does anyone know why? Why would he just skip off like that?" Rose asked, straightening her skirt.

"Well," said Norma, "I'm not one to talk, but if you ask me, he sounds quite independent. Then again, I can't say I blame him. The Jewish Quarter is a mess." Norma put her hand at the side of her mouth, as if that would minimize what she was about to say. "As you know, the search for our mysterious sleeper is in full force. There are some Jews who are suspecting other Jews at this point! No one in the Jewish Quarter has escaped suspicion. Which visitor in his right mind would want to stay here?"

In Sophia's eyes, the compassionate and peaceful air that surrounded Matlub pushed away all possible suspicions from him.

"The next thing I heard, he was missing. Disappeared." Norma popped a whole dried apricot into her mouth. "Well, it's not like he is a local here. He is from Halab." The sticky fruit stuck to her bottom tooth. "Who knows? Maybe he was accused of being the sleeper?"

"But he is a doctor," Sophia said. "What would he want with informing on our community?"

"I am told," Norma said, "that our *Mukhabarat* can create all kinds of lifestyles just to give a sleeper more acceptability, you know, help him blend in more with the community so he doesn't seem suspicious at all. But let's not worry too much about this." Norma released the subject with her finger, as if shooing away a fly.

A concert of crashes sounded from outside. Rose Zalta dropped the dishrags in her hand. Sophia jumped to her feet. Her father swung around.

"Help...he-e-elp," a voice groaned from outside.

They all walked slowly around the window pane and pulled back the curtain. Outside, Huda sat moaning at the bottom of the steps. "Help me. Someone help!" She clutched her leg beneath a toppled ladder.

Sophia ran down the steps.

"Don't touch her!" her mother called. "If anything is broken, you can make it worse."

Huda lay down, sprawled out on the ground. Sophia pulled the ladder off of her. Vines torn from the *hohsh* wall tangled in the ladder. Sophia leaned it against the wall. "Huda, are you alright?"

Huda's head circled wildly and her eyes rolled backward. "A doctor," she whispered.

Jack said he could drive faster than a horse being hunted by a pack of hyenas. Sophia rode in the backseat next to Huda, who had her head resting on Sophia's lap. "Just a little bit longer, Huda," Sophia said reassuringly. She stretched her neck over the front seat. "Can't you go any faster, Jack?"

Jack slowed down. A herd of cattle crossed in front

of the car. He looked up in the rearview mirror. "Just make sure Pharaoh doesn't do anything messy back there," he whispered. "I promised to return this car in perfect condition, as soon as we get her to a doctor."

The doctor. Matlub, the doctor. Regardless of where her thoughts went, they seemed to always end up with him.

"You warm back there?" Jack asked.

"It doesn't matter," Sophia said. Under her breath, she mumbled, "Nothing matters."

"Just turn the knob." He smacked the car panel at his side. "Fine piece of machinery." He honked at the few straggling sheep that lingered behind.

They sped along the rocky streets until the hospital came into view. Jack pulled up in front of the emergency entrance. An attendant peeked in the window after a few minutes and hailed down two orderlies, who lifted Huda onto a canvas stretcher that was held in place by two wooden poles.

Huda was given a bed right away. A nurse escorted Sophia and Jack into a room as noisy as the *souk*. People covered the floor, sitting and standing between the occupied chairs in the waiting room. Sophia and Jack tiptoed between the remaining small gaps on the floor. "I could have brought Huda's cat to keep her company," Jack mumbled to himself. "No one would notice." A rooster ruffled its feathers and jumped noisily inside a big cage on the dirty floor beside its owner. On the other side of the room, a girl screamed on her mother's lap until her mother smacked her across her head. Near her, a man swore beneath the life-size photograph of Haffez-al-Assad, insisting that he was next in line.

Out of the corner of her eye, Sophia caught sight of a man from afar just before he exited the building. She pointed outside. "Doesn't that man look a lot like Matlub?"

Jack turned around. "Out there? Naaa."

The nurse cleared her throat. "Only one person can join me past this door on behalf of the patient. Who will it be?"

"I'll go," Sophia said, pulling her eyes away from where she had just seen the man. She took her place behind the nurse, leaving Jack in the pool of chaos.

By then, Huda had become unconscious and was hooked up to a bunch of wires. "What happened to her?" the nurse asked.

"I think she fell off a ladder," Sophia said. "Or she might have fallen down the stairs."

The nurse continued with the rest of her questionnaire until the machines connected to Huda began sounding off in unison. This immediately brought a team of hospital staff running to her bedside. Sophia stepped back when the nurse threw Huda's chart in the bin on the edge of the bed and joined the rest of the medical team.

After hours of turmoil, Huda, although still in critical condition, was finally stable. Sophia went out into the waiting room and scanned the area for her brother-in-law. She found him slumped over in a chair, snoring.

"Jack," she called, her voice low.

He sat up, startled. "Whaa-?"

"Go home. Huda is stable."

"What about you?" he asked, rubbing the heel of his hand over his eyes.

"I'll stay here," Sophia said. "They gave me a chair beside her bed. I don't want to leave her alone."

"I'll let your father know." Jack straightened up and dragged himself outside.

Sophia returned to Huda. The nurse handed her a blanket and a pillow and pointed to a rattan chair at the foot of the bed.

"You'll be here tonight. We are not taking any chances by moving her, even though she seems stable. Let's just hope your friend wakes up."

"Thank you," Sophia said, settling into the chair.

"I put the patient's belongings in the drawer here - just her clothes and the purse she had tied to her waist. Call the nurse on duty if you notice any change in her. I'm going home; my shift is over. I'll see you both first thing in the morning."

Sophia felt a light tap on her shoulder just as she began to doze off. Her mother pulled up a chair beside her. "Sophia?"

Sophia told her mother about Huda's prognosis. "I'm here anyway, Ma. You might as well go home. I'll try to walk over as soon as I hear something. There is no need for both of us to sleep here."

"You are right. If I get some sleep now, maybe I'll be able to relieve you later."

Sophia awoke the next morning to the stench of camel soup and stale garbage left for the morning cleaning crew. The pattern of rattan had impressed into the back of her legs, and she stood quickly and stretched. Then she washed up and tied her hair neatly with the few supplies offered to her by the night nurse.

The hospital was surprisingly quiet, with only the night shift summing up the last of their reports before transferring their patients to the morning staff. She softly uttered her memorized prayers, being careful to slash her tone each time someone walked past. Speaking the Hebrew language publicly would bring immediate inquiries and accusations of her being a Zionist sympathizer.

When she was finished praying, she sat back down on the chair. She folded the wrinkled sheet she had been given and placed it behind her head. When she closed her eyes and leaned back, Matlub's soft and direct voice echoed inside her mind.

Matlub's name, she knew, meant "the requested". Matlub, the requested. The meaning of his name taunted her. His inner happiness and contentment harassed her. "Where are you, Matlub?" she whispered, squeezing her eyes shut. Her pain sailed from her stomach up to her throat. In a matter of days, her heart had traveled from utter joy to inner confusion, from reviving waters to barren lands, from a new life to expired dreams.

"I know you are not the sleeper, Matlub."

The beeping monitor sounded steadily in the background, but Sophia ignored it, intent on her one-sided conversation with Matlub. "So where are you?" she repeated, her eyes still tightly closed.

"Here," a faint voice responded.

Sophia's eyes flew open. This was not part of her reverie. This wasn't Matlub's voice at all. It was Huda's voice! She looked at the bed, where she saw Huda's eyelids begin to flutter. "I'm here," Huda repeated weakly. "Miss Sophia?"

Sophia sprang to her feet. "Huda? You are up!" She rushed to Huda's side.

Huda struggled to lift her head. "I should have known ... you would be praying for me." She dropped her head and cringed in pain.

"Don't strain yourself," Sophia said. "I'll call someone to help, to lift your back for you." She pushed the button on the wire hanging off the side of Huda's bed.

No one responded. "Keep your eyes open, Huda. Everyone has been waiting for you to wake up." Sophia squinted, peering down the hall. "The morning nurse should be here any minute. You remember her - the nice lady who took care of you when we came in?"

"Where am I?"

"In the hospital."

Huda attempted to look around. "Where in the hospital?" she asked.

"You are in the ward on the first floor, just outside the emergency room, Huda," Sophia replied.

Huda turned her head to the side and spat. "They are supposed to treat me well - a nice room, flowers, everything." She pulled Sophia's sleeve. "Undercover, you get nothing. Do you hear me? Nothing."

Sophia's heart skipped a beat.

"Try and hide a message for the *Mukhabarat* in a cat's fur. Smelly cat ... Serves those Jews right. My son died trying to kill one of them." Huda let go of Sophia and closed her eyes. Within moments, she was back in a deep sleep.

Sophia remained at Huda's bedside, frozen and stunned. Shock mingled with confusion inside her spinning head and she collapsed back into the armchair, eyes closed wearily. *What was Huda talking about?*

Footsteps sounding from behind her suddenly intruded upon her thoughts. At first, Sophia ignored them. If it was the nurse, she would call her if she wanted her.

Only it wasn't the nurse. The nurse, Sophia knew, did not give off the stench of smoke that was slowly enveloping her. Puzzled, she opened her eyes a sliver. A shadowy man moved stealthily around. He glanced at Sophia and then at Huda, as if to confirm that both of them were asleep, before opening the drawer beside the bed. He pulled out Huda's purse and crouched low to the floor while rummaging inside it.

Sophia didn't move while the man peered at Huda's documents, jewelry, and money. Then he pulled out a card from her purse and glided it into his pants pocket. That is when the man's appearance hit Sophia – the big mole on his cheek.

A gust of alarm struck her. Sophia stared at the man and her body went numb. She closed her eyes quickly, afraid that he might discover that she was awake.

Stung by her realization, she recalled her encounter outside the *Mukhabarat* when she had gone out with Matlub. *He put out the cigarette ... his left side faced me and Matlub. The mole was on his left cheek ... just like this man!*

When he left the room, Sophia ran to the small window outside of the emergency ward and watched him leave the hospital and cross the street. It was definitely the same man. And the woman in the *chador* who had walked by him on that night? Could that have been…?

The morning shift came in with the sound of swinging doors and shuffling papers. "Good morning! How's our patient doing?" Sophia recognized the nurse from the day before.

"She is sleeping," Sophia answered, attempting to stifle the panic from her voice.

The nurse pulled up Huda's eyelid with the back of her pencil. "Still sleeping, huh?"

"She opened her eyes for a few minutes and began saying some things, but then fell right back asleep." Sophia glanced over her shoulder where the man with the mole had just exited.

"That is normal. There is no doubt that she is happy to have you here." The nurse put her arm on Sophia's shoulder. "Why don't you go home and get some rest? I'll tell the doctor where to contact you if there is a change in the patient. You can come back later and check in on her."

Sophia's notions became jaded by the nurse's tone. It shrank them and dissipated them into the background of beeping machines, swinging doors, rolling wheelchairs, and dingy hallways.

"Her vitals look a lot better," the nurse continued in that same smooth voice. "We'll have the doctor check on her. She does have some painful-looking bruises, but nothing broken. I'll give her another shot of morphine to keep her calm. Don't get discouraged if she doesn't remember that you came for her."

Sophia allowed herself to get up and follow the

nurse to the door. "You did well, my dear. Now go and get some rest," the nurse told her.

Sophia felt queasy with each step she took toward the hospital exit – closer and closer toward exposing the truth that she had just discovered.

22

Sophia walked home slowly, trying to catalogue the conversations, words, and impressions of the past day. Without her realizing it, she broke her stride into a sprint, then returned to a walk, and then back to a sprint again.

The battered wheels of a passing cart rolled over the jagged stones behind her. She could hear the conversations of the group of workers riding inside the cart. She stepped aside in the narrow road while they passed, feeling their envious eyes, scornful stares, and hateful words – designed for her and all those like her.

Sophia looked down, assuming the humility of a less-than-second-class citizen. One boy rose from his seat on the cart. "Jewish worm!" he yelled, throwing an empty soda can at her head. She dared to turn around and grabbed a broken, rusted pipe that stood against the wall at her side. She dragged it toward the cart and held it above her head. The boy sat down beside his father.

Her tormentors swayed in the distance, rolling further and further away. Her thoughts bled with the continuous struggle of a nation surrounded by hatred that was second nature for the Arab locals. She released the pipe from her hand and kicked it against the wall.

Her heart raced with her discovery. The woman in the *chador*. It had to be Huda. *Huda – the confession she had inadvertently made - the man with the mole – the* Mukhabarat. She remembered her family's open conversations about her brothers, about escape, about the safe routes. Which ones had been recorded? Why her? Why her family?

Once she entered her *hohsh*, she walked into the kitchen, washed up, and changed into a clean dress. Rose Zalta and Grandpa Yosef came in with fruit from the courtyard trees. "Is that you, Sophia?"

"Hi," she said, all traces of life drained from her tone.

Rose released the fruit in her arms. A few rolled off the countertop. "You're back from the hospital. You must be exhausted. How is Huda?"

Apathy possessed her. She stared out the window, motionless.

Grandpa Yosef pulled out a chair for Sophia.

Rose pushed Sophia's hair away from her eyes. "This is so unlike you, Sophia. Are you alright? Is something wrong with Huda?"

Sophia sat down. Grandpa Yosef sat beside her.

Rose tried again. "Alright, let's start with last night.

You took Huda to the hospital with Jack and… "

Sophia looked into Grandpa Yosef's clear blue eyes and sighed. His serenity smiled at her.

Rose kneeled before her daughter. "Talk to me, please, Sophia."

Sophia rubbed her eyes. "Huda is stable; nothing broken."

"That is good," Rose said.

"She did have some internal bleeding. The nurse said that she would recover, probably in full."

"How does she look?" Rose asked.

"Better than last night."

"And?" her grandfather asked.

Sophia shook her foot nervously. Rose stroked her daughter's hand.

"And she opened her eyes for a few minutes. She is coming into consciousness."

"That is terrific," Rose said.

Sophia stood up and looked outside the window. A single bird flew across the courtyard with a twig in its beak. Six more followed, in formation.

"What is it, Sophia?" Grandpa Yosef gently persisted.

Her face tightened while she strained to cushion her words with subtlety. "I think Huda is working undercover for the *Mukhabarat*."

Grandpa Yosef sat back. For a split second, Sophia saw that her words had tampered with his composure.

"What?!" Rose shrieked.

"It all started with Matlub."

Rose held on to a chair before sitting down in it. "Matlub, too?"

"No, no. I'll explain," Sophia went on. "Matlub and I went for a picnic the night we went out. We passed the headquarters of the *Mukhabarat* on the way. A woman in a *chador* had just been walking out. I couldn't see her face because she was already ahead of us, but I could have wagered that it was Huda."

"How could you be sure?" Rose interrupted.

Sophia continued, her thoughts unbroken. "At the same time, two men stood against the side door of the building, smoking. One of them had a big mole on his face. It was creepy. But I forgot about it until today in the hospital."

Grandpa sat up. "What happened in the hospital?"

Sophia turned to him. "When Huda opened her eyes for those few moments, she began mumbling things. First she complained how horrible it is to work undercover, that she doesn't get the respect she deserves. She said she has to hide messages for the *Mukhabarat* in her cat's smelly fur, but that it serves the Jews right ..." Her voice trailed off into a shudder, but she forced herself to continue.

"Then, as soon as Huda fell back asleep, a man reeking of cigarette smoke walked into the room. I was sitting in the chair beside Huda with my eyes closed, so he thought I was asleep. When I opened my eyes a bit, I saw him going through Huda's stuff. I immediately recognized him as the man with the mole on his face. I remember it was on the left side, beneath his cheekbone, just like the man we saw outside the *Mukhabarat*."

"Oh, this is too much!" Rose put her head in her hands. "Huda working undercover?!"

"*Baruch* Hashem, though, Sophia has been able to make sense of her discoveries."

At her grandfather's words, Sophia sat up straighter. "What do you think, Grandpa? Could Huda be our sleeper?"

Grandpa nodded softly. "She might be."

"Are you saying that our Huda has been sweeping stairs and spying on us at the same time?" Rose's complexion turned white.

Sophia shuddered again. "She had access to our lives."

Rose shook her head over and over. "I still don't understand. Huda, the most incapable housekeeper I know, has all along been a sleeper living in our home?"

"In a way, we all knew it, didn't we? From the start we all realized that something was 'off' with her." Grandpa Yosef closed his eyes. "Hashem will help."

"Wait until Father finds out," Sophia said.

Rose rubbed out a small smudge on the table. "He'll be here late tonight."

23

"**Q**uiet!" Shlomo Zalta's voice boomed through the house.

Instantly, the bickering and yelling in the room halted.

"This home will not crumble because of what has transpired." He waved his hand and dismissed any up-coming comments.

Rose dried her hands. "Do you think Huda will know what Sophia has discovered?"

"Are you thinking of keeping her, Mother?" Boomeh tucked the blanket around the baby in her arms.

Rose Zalta massaged her temples. "I don't know. I feel so uncomfortable about the whole thing."

Boomeh set the sleepy baby on the sofa. "Maybe we should ask her what she meant by what she said and why that man went through her things and took something.

Maybe she has a logical explanation for everything."

"That Pharaoh has been a mess from the start," Jack said. Crumbs of *ka'ak* tumbled down the frayed edges of his button-down shirt. "I say get rid of her before she really causes trouble."

Sophia shook the tablecloth out the window.

"What do you think, Grandpa?" Shlomo asked his father-in-law.

Grandpa Yosef straightened a pile of books on the table. He looked up at the faces strained with uncertainty. "Now that Sophia has discovered what the entire community has been tormented over, we should be celebrating. At least we know what we have here. We have found our sleeper. If we don't welcome her back, who will they bring in her stead? And to whom? And how will we feel then?"

Everyone sat back, digesting Grandpa's words.

Sophia's father cleared his throat. "Grandpa is right. Jack, you notify the men at the *k'nees*. Tell everyone to beware. Let them know about Huda. Remember, we don't want her to suspect that we know anything. Like Grandpa said, we are comfortable with our sleeper. We don't need to send her away for them to bring us a new one."

Not everyone understood the idea of keeping Huda. Some of the men from the *bet hakenesset* were happy and thanked Jack for containing Huda to his home. Others were upset that Huda had access to the Jewish Quarter altogether.

The news spread. The vague comments about the sleeper being discovered comforted the community. The sleeper was identified as a Muslim – just a Muslim.

"I wonder why Matlub just picked up and left," Sophia said to her mother in the kitchen the next day.

Sophia's mother reached into the laundry basket and pressed out a shirt in her lap. "Maybe we didn't try hard enough to find out why."

"Would it have helped?" Grandpa asked, overhearing. "If no one can find him, there must be a reason why he doesn't want to be seen."

"I guess you are right. But in a way, I am selfish." Rose Zalta picked up a dishrag from the basket and held it at the side of her mouth. "I can't help it," she whispered to her father. "He was the only one she was ever interested in."

"She knows exactly what she needs. That is a good thing."

Rose looked over at Sophia and sighed. Sophia kept her head in the book she pretended to be reading, secretly adding her sorrow to theirs.

Rose pressed down the pile in the basket. "I'll get to that later," she said. She pulled off her apron and peeked into the corner where Sophia sat. "I may need your help tonight, Sophia."

Sophia looked up. Her face softened with defeat.

"Another birth. It could be any day, but I have a feeling it will be tonight," Rose said. "What do you think?"

By now, Sophia had become known in the community as the midwife's assistant, gaining respect and compliments with each satisfied customer. The mothers loved how calming she was and requested that Sophia stay in the room for their births. With her sharp eye and efficiency, she followed Rose's techniques and the soothing way in which she handled the mothers.

During each birth, Sophia took as many burdens as she could off of her mother, and with her diligence, her mother gave her more responsibilities, so that she knew just about everything there was to know about midwifery. She made a name for herself in the way she combined her herbs for massages with each birth. One mother called Rose and Sophia "Shifrah and Puah," after the heroines in the Torah, Yocheved and Miriam, who assisted in the births of the Jewish people despite the evil decrees of King Pharaoh.

Rose went over to her daughter and put her arm around her shoulder. Sophia leaned her head against her mother and heaved a big sigh.

"There is something else that ensures our success at each birth – and throughout each day." Rose gave her daughter a meaningful look. "It is called *siyata d'Shmaya* - Heavenly assistance. Things are going to be good." Rose patted her softly. "You'll see."

Sophia closed the book on her lap, hoping to cut out Matlub from her mind.

24

"I've never seen anything like that," Rose said after they came in the next morning.

Sophia pulled off the cotton mask from around her neck. "I'm going to lie down for a little bit."

"Not yet," Rose Zalta said. "Give me that mask. Give me your clothes, too. We have to boil everything. Then you scrub for a long time in that bath."

"Can't I do that later? I'm so tired."

"Sophia Zalta! We just came out of a Bedouin camp hit with typhoid. It's a good thing we were far away from the plagued tent. I know you are exhausted, but you don't take chances with typhoid! I'll pour the hot water. I'll take care of everything. You just make sure everything you take off goes into this bucket, alright?"

"I know." Sophia set the bucket next to the big copper pot they called a bath. "Make sure no one comes in."

"I'm staying right here. Don't you worry," Rose told her.

Sophia closed the curtain, cutting off the big copper pot in the corner of the kitchen.

"I'm sorry about today," Rose said. "I thought this was a birth of someone in the *haret* who just happened to live outside the Jewish Quarter. When we finally got closer to the tents, I was afraid to turn back. You never know what the authorities would make of it, you know, refusing to aid an Arab. They did pay nicely, though." Rose slid another pitcher of hot water beneath the curtain in front of the bath. "How are you doing in there?"

"Fine, Mother. I don't want to get out."

Rose laughed. "I'll heat some more water." She stretched her own tired limbs. "I never thought that midwifery would be anything more than a kindness. Now, we actually need that money."

"It's kind of nice without Huda making background noise in the kitchen."

"Don't get so comfortable," Rose said. "She'll be back soon."

"Today?" A ball of fury rose up inside Sophia.

"Remember what Grandpa Yosef said. He's right. We have no choice. We have to take her in, at least for now," Rose responded.

"I keep hoping that something bad happens to her on the way home from the hospital. I keep hoping she never makes it here! Is that terrible?"

"Shhh! Don't tempt the Satan!"

Later that afternoon, Rose stood on a chair and

hooked a purple sheet onto a rusty nail above her head. "Huda always liked this color. Maybe it will seem festive to her, like we are glad to have her back, if we drape it here and there. Your father doesn't want her suspecting that we know anything." She turned to her daughter holding the chair below. "You do it, Sophia. I just can't bear it!" she whimpered.

Sophia pulled the chair against the wall and yanked the fabric into a rope. "We can welcome her back, but do we have to hang fabric on the wall as if I were engaged?"

"I know exactly what you mean," Rose said. "But just do it."

"I thought about a great plan when we left the Bedouin camp today. If enough people die in there, maybe an entire family, we can all fake our deaths, all of us."

"Sophia!" her mother responded in shock.

Grandpa Yosef looked up, allowing his eyeglasses to fall onto his lap.

"Then," Sophia continued, "We can all leave this place – without questions, without consequences."

Shlomo slammed his hand on the table. "Young lady, that will be enough! Now, listen to your mother. At the same time, we all have to be a little bit more cautious around here. Especially about what we say." He shot Sophia a look. "We cannot give Huda any reason to go snooping around. It has to be …"

"Boring!" Sophia threw an orange into the air and caught it with one hand.

Grandpa Yosef chuckled.

"Put that down," Shlomo said to her.

Sophia plopped into a chair. "Maybe we should have a sign, some way for everyone to know that Huda is here. I can't behave all day like my every move is being recorded."

"You can and you will!"

"A sign to warn people when Huda is coming?" Grandpa Yosef said. "That would be interesting."

Jack jumped up. "I'll be right back." Upon returning, he raised his hand and cleared his throat. "Attention please. Sorry to intrude, everyone. We still have some time, though."

"Time?" Shlomo asked.

"Yes, time. Time to prepare us all before Pharaoh walks into this *hohsh*." Jack handed everyone what looked like a stout twig with a string running through it. He pulled the last one up to his mouth and blew into it. "Weeeeoeeeew!" the mock birdcall screeched through the *hohsh*.

Grandpa Yosef held his up to the light.

"What exactly is this for?" Shlomo asked.

Jack picked up the whistle hanging around his neck. "This is an emergency whistle. This will be our signal. When one of us blows on it, the rest of us will know that Pharaoh is coming and we must all beware."

Everyone stared at Jack.

"Don't be afraid," Jack told them. "This is a way to prepare ourselves, for our own protection. Wear it around your necks, everyone. Wear it and never take it off."

Sophia sniffed the raw scent from inside the whistle and blew on it. "Won't Huda hear it, too?"

"Everything we do seems strange to Huda," Rose said.

"She could think it is a modern shofar if she wants to," Grandpa said, "but she will most likely think it is meant to ward off the evil eye."

Jack eyed the courtyard from the window. "We can't be too careful anymore. Not with Huda and not with any-one."

25

"Sophia! Time to get ready! We don't want to be late," Rose Zalta called down the hall the next morning.

The front door closed. Shlomo Zalta walked into the front hall.

"There you are," Rose said. "I haven't seen you all morning. I was beginning to worry."

"They called me down to the *Mukhabarat*," Shlomo said to his wife.

"The *Mukhabarat*?" Sophia asked, surprising them both with her presence.

Rose shooed her back to her room and continued speaking with her husband. "What for?" she whispered. "What did they want?"

"They said they just wanted to talk."

Rose put her hand over her mouth and sat down

slowly in a chair. "Talk? About what? You don't look too good. Shlomo?"

"They didn't do anything. One of the agents offered me a cigar and asked me if I knew about the recent escape. He asked about my family and whether or not we were loyal to the Arab nation."

"What else happened?" Rose pressed.

Shlomo sat beside his wife. "He reminded me that any information about these escapes belonged to the Syrian government."

"What did you say?"

"I told him that I understood completely. He asked me again if I had anything to share with him. I told him no, and that was it."

"Just like that?" Rose asked.

"Just like that," Shlomo said, nodding silently.

"Did they mention Huda or anything else?"

"No, and neither did I. Let's hope that this is the end of it."

"I worry though, Shlomo," Rose said, her voice shaking.

"Let's pray for the best, Rose. We can't do much more than that."

Rose stood and pulled the apron off from around her neck. "We had better leave soon. Come on, Sophia! We don't want to be late for Jacob's bar mitzvah."

Shlomo Zalta smacked his hands together. "Let's go."

Sophia walked back into the room, directing her fearful expression at her father. She did not find what she was looking for. The strength had already left his countenance.

"Sophia, please remind Boomeh and Jack that we are leaving now," her mother said. "It would be nice if we all left together, yes?"

Sophia ran down the steps. Her white sweater puffed up behind her with the cool morning air.

Grandpa Yosef stood up outside, folded a paper into his book, and pushed the book into the inside pocket of his jacket. "You must be looking forward to this day," he told Sophia.

"Yes, Grandpa. I really am."

✷　✷　✷

They walked into the Franj Synagogue together. Eva's family was there already to celebrate Jacob's bar mitzvah. Inside, Jacob carried the *sefer* Torah in his arms and set it down on the *bimah* in the center of the sanctuary. His father, who had been guiding him, came by his side. Ululant cries came from the women's section. Sophia waved to Eva and Eva waved back.

For his bar mitzvah, Jacob stood by his father as his father read a portion from the Torah reading that week. Afterward, Jacob finished the mishnayot he had prepared for his *siyum* and recited the *hadran*. Eva's mother kept dabbing at her tear-soaked face with a handkerchief. Jacob read with pure concentration. When he was done, the audience roared. No one said a word about his blindness.

Women threw *lebas* into the air. One of them hit Sophia's father in the head. Jacob laughed at the sounds of all the fuss everyone was making over him.

The bar mitzvah was a success. Light *mazza* was served for the occasion. No one needed it. They were all filled with the satisfaction and the understanding that Hashem takes care of all of His children.

Sophia tapped Eva on the shoulder. "You are glowing."

"So much has happened," Eva whispered. "I need to speak to you."

Sophia backed into a corner. "What?"

Eva leaned in closer. "I have my fourth meeting tonight with the *same* boy."

"Really, Eva? That's terrific!"

"I think he may be the one. I'm not sure if he sees it yet, though. He may be a little afraid of commitment. At least that is what the *dallaleh* said. She had to convince him to go out each time. I don't care, though. Benny is so nice and I am really happy when we are together."

"Benny?" Sophia yelped.

"Not so loud." Eva looked over her shoulder. "His father, the butcher, was somewhere here."

"The butch–" Sophia choked on her words.

"Are you alright?" Eva ran to get her a cup of water.

"I'm fine." Sophia's voice trailed like a thin piece of thread.

"Good," Eva said. "Wish me luck."

Sophia cleared her throat. "I wish you more than that." She closed her eyes tightly. "Hashem should bless you and your *naseeb* that you should recognize each other with clarity and with ease, and your lives should be filled with happiness and health and success."

"Amen!" Eva hugged Sophia. "Thank you."

Later, Sophia blamed herself for being completely unaware of the disaster that had been taking place the entire time.

26

Grandpa Yosef was the first one to sense that some-thing was very wrong. At least that was the way it seemed. "Walk slowly," he urged them. "The day is nice." Sophia listened as Grandpa told stories of his childhood that took place in the very same streets of the Jewish Quarter. He pointed to homes of his old friends and to the corners and crossings most favored by his generation. It was the slowest walk she had ever taken back to her home.

The courtyard looked the same. Sophia turned around, sensing that there was someone watching her, expecting her. Rose opened the door to the house. "Oh, my! Oh, my!" she said over and over again. Sophia's father flung open the front door.

"Just look at this place!"

Sophia jumped over the drawers sprawled by the entrance. The end table had been thrown over onto its side. The Persian rugs had been turned over, jugs and silver dishes hung out of the dining room cabinet, and pots, utensils, and broken dishes were piled high on the floor in the front room.

"Who would do this?" Boomeh asked, clutching her baby.

Jack stuck his head out the window.

"It was those men, wasn't it, Father?" Sophia said, kicking over a corner of the Persian rug.

"What men?" Jack asked.

"From the *Mukhabarat*," Sophia said. "The ones you met today."

"Don't even say that word," Rose said. She collected a path of scattered papers. Shlomo took them from her.

Sophia quickly turned over the end table and closed the drawers to the cabinet. "Is this because of me? Because of my complaining about living here?" she asked her father.

"With all your ideas," Jack said.

Grandpa Yosef shot a look at Jack and weaved around the chairs on the floor.

"There is no place for blame here," Shlomo said.

"They were obviously looking for something, though," Grandpa remarked.

"Probably something Huda had seen." Sophia looked out into the courtyard. "Who else would have told them?"

"Unless Huda herself did this," Jack began.

"That is doubtful," Boomeh replied. She rocked the baby in her arms. "Huda is recovering in the hospital."

One by one, they picked up the pieces of their home and tried to make sense of it again.

"Maybe she saw what I gave you, Father, you know, the drawing that I thought was a map. I don't remember putting it away."

Shlomo didn't answer.

"I should have known that they wouldn't stop at just questioning Father." Sophia picked up two halves of a broken vase. "I should have stayed behind."

"That would have been even more dangerous," Grandpa Yosef said, brushing Boomeh's baby's cheek with his hand. "As long as we are safe."

"I have decided," Shlomo announced, "that today, young lady, you will be staying home. No leaving the house today, or tomorrow, or ever, until I say so. Is that clear?"

"But Father, why?"

"Is that clear?"

Sophia nodded. Everyone stood quietly.

"Let's concentrate on moving forward," Grandpa Yosef continued. "There must be something next on our list of things to do."

Rose handed Sophia a broom. "After straightening up here," she said, "I can think of a thing or two."

Sophia reluctantly swept the floor.

"I'll set up the heavy things that need to be moved," Jack offered.

"I'm going to put the baby to sleep," Boomeh said.

"That's more like it," Grandpa said, nodding his head. "And I'll help Sophia."

Shlomo Zalta looked around the room. "I guess I'll go work on a stronger lock for the *hohsh* door."

"Who is going to look out for Huda?" Boomeh asked before leaving the room. "She should be back by now."

Jack followed Boomeh out. "She probably stayed at the hospital on purpose."

The pace in their house quickened until just about everything was back in its place. Grandpa Yosef stretched a tapestry over the new gash in the wall. Sophia helped him hang it on the hook. "What do you think they were looking for in here?" she asked him.

The sound of Jack's whistle pierced the air. Sophia ran to the window.

"The bird call," Grandpa announced.

"Grandpa is right!" Sophia pulled herself up onto the window frame and balanced on the sill. "Look over there, on top of the wall. It's Jack!"

"Do you think he sees Huda?" Rose asked.

"From up there, he can see just about anything," Grandpa Yosef responded, stretching to see for himself what was happening outside.

Sophia adjusted the purple fabric that hung on one side above the doorway.

Her father suddenly walked in. "What are you doing, young lady?"

"Just fixing this. Huda is back, and she doesn't know that I witnessed her friend from the *Mukhabarat* paying her a visit. Hopefully, she won't remember our conversation either. Ma said we should keep it that way. This fabric is for her welcoming home party. She should believe that everything is the same between us."

Shlomo shook his head. "I can't believe this."

Grandpa Yosef patted Shlomo's shoulder. "Just sit back and watch, Shlomo."

The ambulance stopped at the gates of the Jewish Quarter. The driver wheeled Huda through the narrow alleys. Jack blew his whistle and scrambled around the *hohsh*. "Everyone act normal! As if nothing happened. Huda is coming. Huda is here." He knocked over a lamp and tripped on the corner of the silk carpet. Even Grandpa Yosef chuckled.

Shlomo whisked Sophia down the hall. "Sophia, it would be a good idea for you to go to your room now."

"My room? Why?"

"Take a rest."

"But I feel fine. I was going to help Huda up the steps."

"In your room, now!"

"First I can't leave the house, and now I can't even leave my room?" Sophia mumbled, stricken by her father's inexplicable harshness.

Minutes later, Huda walked through the front door.

"Huda!" Rose called out. "Welcome back!"

Huda looked around and smiled.

"How are you feeling?" Rose asked.

"A little better each day," Huda replied with a grimace. She limped down the hall toward Sophia's bedroom. "Was that you, Miss Sophia? They told me you stayed with me in the hospital."

Shlomo stood in Huda's path. "She's not feeling so

well. Looks like a fever. Wouldn't want you to catch anything, especially while you are still recuperating from your fall."

"It is so nice for you to remember to thank Sophia, Huda, although you know that it was her pleasure to be there for you," Rose said, taking Huda's arm and turning her around.

"I really don't remember a thing. Just that I was in so much pain. I hadn't felt pain like that since my husband threw me down the stairs, oh, over twenty years ago."

"You don't remember seeing Sophia?" Rose asked.

"I can't recall anything. The nurses filled me in on what happened, but let me think now a minute ..."

"No, no," Rose said, trying to distract her. "Don't you think about a thing now, except for the future and your complete recovery."

Sophia opened the door a crack. She caught a glimpse of her mother as she whisked Huda into the decorated front room filled with music and jubilant cries. Her eye moved on to Grandpa Yosef as he pulled at the strings of his *oud* and played a whiny tune, then on to Boomeh as she clapped her hands, then back to Rose, who was now throwing *lebas* into the air, and on to Jack as he walked in, blowing the whistle designated to signal the coming of Huda. Shlomo Zalta waved on, and the sharpness of his smile nearly pinched her. At last, her eye caught the purple fabric draped over the front door – her reminder of the confinement she was expected to live with and the danger they were all now being forced to celebrate.

27

For days, her father forbade her to leave her bedroom. No one was permitted to enter, except for her mother and father themselves. No one was to mention Sophia's well-being. Her father made no attempt to explain himself, either. Rose Zalta sighed each time a confused and angry Sophia begged her to get out for just a little sunlight, especially on the day Eva came to call on her, but all she said to Sophia was, "Your father is doing the right thing, even though it may be difficult to see that right now. Just trust him."

Huda was excused from all her household duties. "Bed-rest and fresh air are the doctor's orders," Boomeh constantly reminded her. Huda never questioned Boomeh, as she hated to work anyway, and she didn't want to go near whatever it was that Sophia had contracted.

Sophia did have a game of *toleh* to keep herself busy,

although she was forced to play for both sides. She couldn't remember having ever slept as much as she did during those few days. There was simply nothing else to do. She slept so much that day seemed like night to her – until that night. It was still dark when her mother came to her bedside and shook her awake.

"Quickly, Sophia. Wake up! Please, wake up."

Sophia slipped out of bed and followed her mother cautiously to the front room. Even though it had only been a few days since she had left her room, Sophia looked around the white walls of her house as if seeing them for the first time. Her father closed the curtains on the window and turned around. Worry added lines to the creases on his forehead. The serious look on his face made him look ten years older.

"What is it, Father?"

"There was a girl from the Bedouin camp. She was left to tend to her family's herd and never returned home. They finally found her, sick with typhoid and unconscious, alone in a deserted field. She died soon after, even before they had a chance to get her to a doctor."

"The plague has been spreading," Sophia said. "Ma and I were just there, and we saw for ourselves."

Rose rubbed her hands together uneasily. "Some say it was the Jews who poisoned the water."

"Yes, yes, Rose, but let's concentrate on our plan," Shlomo said.

"Plan? What plan?" Sophia asked.

"I don't know, Shlomo. This whole thing is making me very nervous," Rose said.

"She will never have this opportunity again," Shlomo insisted. "Let's just tell her."

"Alright, alright!" Rose resigned herself to a chair.

Shlomo continued speaking. "The girl's family is willing to give her body over to us – for a price, of course."

Sophia stared. "What are you saying, Father?"

Shlomo grabbed hold of his daughter. "Do you hear me? The family is willing to sell the deceased girl to us in exchange for money and a decent burial. Everyone will think she is you. She is your age and has dark hair, just like you. *This* is your chance! Your only chance for escape!"

"Escape? Father, how will I? What if they find out?"

"You have been seen in the Bedouin camp assisting a birth. You have also been in solitary confinement for days now. Huda is our witness. They can't do anything to us. They won't even want to come near our house if there is a chance that it has been touched with typhoid."

In just seconds, her father's words had dissolved the pain and confusion that had cultivated in her mind these past few days. "That's why you kept me locked up all this time?" Sophia could not restrain the pure admiration from her tone.

"We took the chance and planned for the possibility. Hashem took care of the rest." Her father inhaled deeply. "There will be a car in the marketplace to take you and a few other people. Gazeem swore to me on his life that this smuggler is reliable and not under the influence of the *Mukhabarat*. He can get you into Lebanon. When you get there, go see the rabbi in the Magen Abraham Synagogue of Beirut. He can arrange to get you out of the country.

Most of the people he helps to escape end up in the Aretz. That is the plan. Now, it's up to you."

Sophia never imagined that the one thing she had always hoped for would be too big for her to consider, so much so, that she fumbled with her thoughts just trying to harness the very idea in her mind.

"Look at her, Shlomo," Rose burst out. "How could we even suggest such a thing for a single girl, out there, all on her own?"

"Isn't this what you have been wanting all along?" her father asked her.

"Yes, it is, but what about you, Father, and you, Mother? What will they do if they find out?"

"No one will know. We are going to display a complete funeral for all of Syria to see, with crying and all. Only, the tears will be real, young lady, as your presence will be missed by all of us."

Rose sat down and sobbed.

Her father's words pulled her closer to the only life she had ever known – her life with her precious family in Syria.

"It will be alright, Rose," Shlomo said. "I will go down to the morgue to identify the body tonight and proceed with all of the necessary arrangements as soon as Sophia ..."

"What do you think, Sophia?" Rose asked her, sniffling. "Honestly."

Sophia held her mother's hand. "Hashem brings us extraordinary opportunities now and then. Maybe this is an opportunity I cannot ignore."

Shlomo smiled at his daughter. "We will pray that this is the right opportunity," he said.

Grandpa Yosef rose from the dark corner. Sophia hadn't even noticed him until then. Turning to him, she said, "Maybe this is my chance, Grandpa, the one I am supposed to be taking."

Grandpa Yosef nodded. "You have always known what you want. Please take this." He handed her his *sefer* Tehillim."

"It's yours, Grandpa." Sophia clutched it to her heart. "I will cherish it forever."

Grandpa closed his eyes and concentrated deeply. "May Hashem light your way and give you complete protection and success always."

Rose's sobs increased at the confirmation of Sophia's decision.

"That is enough, Rose. You'll wake up Huda!" Shlomo whispered.

"Don't tempt the Satan!" Rose took a deep breath and got up. She opened the closet, pulled down a *chador* and veil, and slipped it over Sophia's head.

Sophia took in all of the faces looking at her, trying to capture all she'd be forced to leave behind. "I can't believe I am doing this," she said.

Her father pressed his eyelids shut, but the tears escaped anyway.

Rose hugged her daughter tightly.

Shlomo Zalta wiped his eyes. "Let her go, Rose. There is not much time."

"How will I know which car is the one?" Sophia asked.

"It's the one with a single headlight on low, the right headlight to be specific." Her father handed her an envelope. "This is for the smuggler. And this ," he slipped her a small sack of money, closed tightly with a rubber band, "keep on you, for yourself, just in case. Hashem be with you." Shlomo brushed her cheek.

"Thank you, Father," she said, her words absorbed by the sobs stuck in her throat.

"Boomeh is still up," her mother said, rubbing her shoulder nervously. "Make your goodbye quick."

When a tear released itself from Grandpa Yosef's eye, Sophia closed her eyes and quickly left. Then she turned to take one last look at everything she had ever known and cared deeply for. "Goodbye..." She pulled the black veil over her face and rushed out the door and down the steps, without even looking at what lay ahead of her.

Huda's in the courtyard. The realization hit her as she reached the bottom of the steps. She judged the space between them, trying to calculate how long it would take for Huda to reach her. Huda had just entered and was striding toward the servants' quarters, her black robe snaking behind her. It was too late to go back up the steps. Sophia tried inching into the shadows of the fig trees to alter the timing, to change the point of impact, but she had no time. Any second now, Huda would look up and discover her.

The gap between them shortened. There was nowhere for her to hide. Sophia peered into the stillness, about to announce herself, to do something, anything to break this intensifying fear, even if it meant ruining her chances in the process.

A door slammed suddenly behind her. It was Jack, thrashing through the courtyard. "I'll get you!" he screamed, running toward Huda. "You came to steal again! You Bedouins keep breaking in here!"

"No, it's me! It's Huda!" Huda screamed, cowering to the floor.

Sophia caught herself and held back.

"I don't believe you. If it's really you, Huda, then show me where you sleep."

"Here, here!" Huda stumbled to the servants' quarters with Jack towering over her. He blew the whistle around his neck a few times to distract her even further. Then he spun his head around, spotting Sophia in the shadows and giving her an imperceptible nod. Alerted, she leaped over the tree roots, knowing that Jack had gone out of his way to signal her, to help her. She could not stop to thank him. She could not even see her sister and her baby one last time.

28

It was late enough for the expected hush to cover the marketplace. Her footsteps mixed with cigarette butts and squashed tomatoes. Her shoes became sullied with soot and the stems of string beans discarded by Arab women who had been squatting over their dinner preparations on the curb that day. Shadows darkened nearby walls where faded ink and adhesive had remained from posters and slogans of the decade. Against a nearby gate, a man stared steadily at Sophia.

A single headlight shone from behind a pile of splintered crates. Sophia hastened toward the light. Sudden footsteps echoed behind her. She didn't turn around right away. She lengthened her stride, for the footsteps overlapped each other and sounded light and far.

The man leaning against the nearby gate edged forward and advanced toward her. The footsteps echoed closer and closer – those of the man rushing toward her and those of the people behind breaking into a run. Sophia quickly turned around.

The man from the gate pulled out his revolver. The footsteps from behind, belonging to two teenage girls, caught up with her. The man pointed them toward the car shining with one headlight. "Do you have the money?"

The envelope her father gave her shifted beneath her sleeve.

The smuggler slammed his hand on the car. "No one gets into the car without the money!"

The two teenage girls quickly handed over their share. He opened the door to let them in. Sophia pulled out her share hesitantly when she realized that she had already submitted herself to whatever lay ahead. She had done so the moment she left her *hohsh* that night. The threesome waited in the back seat while the man counted his payment behind the wheel, beside his partner.

Sophia put her hand into the pocket of her *chador* and curled the edges of Grandpa Yosef's Tehillim. The two sisters eyed each other beside her. She remembered them from the *haret*, although she knew they were older, as each had graduated her school already. She watched them, trying not to think of Linda and her sister.

The car pulled out of the marketplace without lights.

"Heads down!" The smuggler screamed over the front seat as he swerved through an intersection in the main road.

Sophia threw her head over her knees. Blood rushed to her head and her back throbbed from pressure. They stayed that way until they reached the Barada River.

"That was good, master," the man's partner said to him as they drove past the city view. "As smooth as the other night when we moved all those guns."

The younger sister beside Sophia gasped.

The man hit his partner with his gun. "No talking, remember."

The partner rubbed his chest. "Okay, master, whatever you say."

It was safe to sit up. Sophia lifted herself vertebrae by vertebrae.

The car rolled slowly until it came to a stop by the river's edge, beside a picnic table.

"Why are we stopping?"

The smuggler ignored Sophia's question and opened the car door.

His partner loaded his gun and turned around. "Not to worry, *Musawi*."

The smugglers proceeded to cover the car with branches and shrubs from the river's edge.

"What are they doing?" the younger sister asked, pulling at her sister.

Sophia rubbed the foggy window. "It looks like they are trying to hide the car."

"Where are we?" the older sister whispered.

The smuggler tapped Sophia's window with his gun and waved at them to come out. Together, the smugglers pushed the car into the bushes until it was fairly camouflaged.

"No shawls!" he barked at the sisters. "Leave your traveling clothes by the river. We are supposed to be hiking teenagers."

They walked on past the river's edge, into the Anti Lebanon Mountains. Sophia's head was in perpetual motion, assessing the smuggler in the front and his partner in the rear. It became harder to keep track of everyone while they climbed the higher peaks. At times, Sophia found herself alone, with only the echoes of panting breaths and scuffling footsteps to keep her on track. Her eyes hurt from straining them to see what poisonous creature lay inside each deep crevice that she grabbed hold of and stepped into.

They passed a small village embraced by the mountain range. There, the villagers kept to themselves, ignoring a victorious escape here or a brutal misfortune there. Hours later, her feet began to blister and ache while she hiked after the smuggler in the lead. The pain pricked her bones enough to quell her fears of escaping. Even the thrilling hint of freedom visited her now and then.

When they had finally reached their halfway mark through the mountains, the leader stopped to finish up his drink while the rest caught up to him. The sisters, who had been trailing Sophia, rested on a rock, their faces drawn with exhaustion. The partner met up with the smuggler and they pointed out their route.

The smuggler tossed his leather skin onto the ground. "Leee's go," he said, slurring his words.

The partner snatched the pouch and sniffed it. "You're drinking *araq* this whole time?" He elbowed the smuggler. "How are we going to get out of here? I don't know the rest of the way."

"Relax!" the smuggler yelled, throwing himself off

balance. "You've come this way before. Besides, I can do this route with my eyes closed."

Sophia took a deep breath, stepping closer to the sisters. She reached into her pocket and rubbed against the *sefer* Tehillim that her grandfather had given her.

"I think I want my money now," the partner said.

"You do, don't you?

"Just give me my share. That's all I am asking for."

"Well, I haven't finished collecting yet." The smuggler stood erect. "All of you!" He headed for Sophia and the sisters. "Hand over your jewelry."

The younger sister began to whimper.

"Do what he says," the older one insisted.

Sophia tossed her bracelet and ring onto the ground at the smuggler, leaving her gold bangles and money where she had tied them to her arm. "*Ein od milbado.* There is nothing else but You, Hashem. Please help us," she whispered over and over.

"Everything!" the smuggler blasted.

The sisters rubbed their hands over their necks and arms. "We gave you everything."

The partner groveled on the ground, scraping up whatever shimmered in the darkness.

The smuggler turned his back on his partner. "There is your share!"

"What about the money?" The partner stuffed his pockets with the jewelry and ran after the smuggler.

Sophia pulled at the sisters. "Stand back."

The smuggler walked on.

His partner balanced his gun and grabbed it by the tip.

"No!" Sophia yelled, in an attempt to save the drunken smuggler, for he was the only one who knew the safe route.

It was too late. By the time the smuggler caught Sophia's warning, his partner had already struck him across the back of his head. Sophia watched in horror as the smuggler dropped instantly to the earth.

29

Her heart thumping painfully in her chest, Sophia stepped in closer to see if the smuggler was alive. He stirred for a second and then went still again. The sisters cowered behind, sobbing softly.

The partner kicked the smuggler's boot and then bent over to check his pulse. "He'll be alright. He's lucky I didn't kill him when he turned his back on me." He reached into the pocket of the still body and grabbed the envelope of money. Then he spat at the smuggler and walked away in the direction they had come from.

"Where are you going?" Sophia called out, following him in the darkness.

"Back home. I have my money. I'm done here."

Sophia slid on a patch of gravel. "What about the rest of us?"

"Lead them yourself, *Musawi*." His spit sprayed Sophia's hand. She wiped her hand on her skirt over and over, but the feeling of it remained.

Sophia pursued him. "But none of us know the way."

The partner lifted his gun. Sophia backed away, watching in silence as he walked off. With her eyes, she followed his gloomy figure bobbing in the night as he took with him the slightest chance they had left of crossing the border safely. She watched until he disappeared behind a mountain.

Visions of baby Aharon's *brit milah* flashed before her. The happiness on her family's faces appeared. Then all of their faces fell into sadness before her as she imagined their display at her staged funeral. Sophia kicked a rock in front of her. It rolled right up to the smuggler and knocked his arm. For a minute he tossed and groaned. Then he went still and quiet again.

"He probably will wake up, but not now," Sophia told the girls. "Even if he would have the strength to get up, he'll stay where he is for a while because of all that *araq* he just finished."

"I should have known this was wrong from the beginning," the older sister said.

"I'm freezing!" The younger sister's voice was at a high shrill. "We'll never get out of here. And even if we do, they'll catch us and kill us!" She broke down, her wailing echoing in the mountains.

Her sister shook her. "Shh! They'll hear you!"

"Who?" the younger sister wailed even louder.

"She's right. There's no one here." Shivering, Sophia blew hot air into her cold cupped hands and rubbed them together.

"But that man lying there, he will wake up? You said it yourself," the older of the sisters begged Sophia.

"He might. But what will he do when he does wake up and get sober? Remember, he doesn't have our money anymore. That may make him real angry. Why would he want to continue helping us?" Sophia slumped onto a rock, stiffening as Grandpa's *sefer* Tehillim in her pocket jabbed into her. She leaned to the side and pulled it out. The moon reflected against the white pages. For a split second, she looked up at the full round moon that, she was sure, was sent especially for her.

"What are you doing?" the older sister asked.

"*L'David mizmor...*" Sophia held the *sefer* up to the light of the moon, her words steady and clear.

The girls slowly joined in, in the shadow of the smuggler's body, repeating the prophetic words of David Hamelech. Sophia passed her finger over Grandpa Yosef's writing on the side of one of the pages. If only she could speak to her wise grandfather now! What would he tell her to do? She unconsciously flipped through the well-worn pages until she hit the inside of the back cover. A drawing on the back cover suddenly caught her eye. She peered at its lines, bending over in an effort to find a beginning and an end.

"What have you got there?" the older sister asked.

"I'm not sure." Sophia curled the corner of the drawing, and saw that it lifted off the back cover as she fiddled with it. With the paper in her hand, she could see that it was folded in half. Opening it, Sophia found a magnified duplicate of the tiny original she had been studying before.

The younger sister, teeth chattering, cuddled up to her sister. "I'm really getting cold."

Sophia followed her finger through the gates and the mountains on the drawing until she stopped at a sea with stick figures of boats and people. "The map—"

The older sister jumped. "Map?"

The map in the cellar! Sophia thought to herself. *It really* had *been a map, not a little child's drawing! And it had been Grandpa Yosef who had placed it there! He must have been the one who had moved it underneath the vat before I found it again and showed it to Father.* Sophia leaped from the rock and climbed up a hill on the side of the mountain, the map flapping in her grip. She plastered the creases of the drawing over a hard surface that overlooked the lower mountains of the range in order to see the details more clearly.

The sudden realization of her grandfather as an international culprit and on the *Mukhabarat's* most-wanted list captured her thoughts – the legendary man holding the safe routes. He had probably helped her brothers escape, too. Her inner laughter surfaced in a smile and then tears. "It was you, Grandpa. All along, it had been you." She licked the sand off her lips. In her black *chador*, she thought of Huda spying on her family and wondered if Huda had ever realized how close she really was.

The sisters called for her from below. Sophia flipped around on her knees in search of a landmark to match the drawing. Then she ran down the incline, almost knocking the sisters over in her excitement. She pointed to an unidentified marking. "Here!"

"Where? What are you saying?"

Sophia tripped over her words. "Through those … two mountains … just about thirty meters down … that way … over the small hill … I … the one I was on."

"What is she saying?"

Sophia took a deep breath to calm herself. She lifted her gaze, setting up a mental route in a place she had never been before. "We should stay as high up as possible to avoid the bandits and Bedouins." She folded the map on its crease. "With Hashem's help, we will get there."

"Get where?" the older sister asked.

"Who is going to help us?" the younger sister asked.

Sophia smiled at them. "*B'ezrat* Hashem, we will finish this escape with or without the smugglers."

The older sister didn't look convinced. "I don't know. Maybe we should have followed the partner back home … asked him if he'd at least take us there…"

The younger sister panicked. "Now it's too late for that, too! Help!"

Sophia grabbed hold of the two sisters and looked them in the eyes. "This is a map of a safe route to Beirut. We have to try it. It is our only chance."

30

They traveled for hours more on foot. The night turned colder and even Sophia's voice began to take on a dismal tone. They had no assurances that they were traveling in the right direction except that Grandpa Yosef's map said so.

Sophia led the sisters through the mountain range, helping them keep up, so that by the time the dawn began to give the sky over to the deep rays of the sun, they all stood together overlooking the rounded hillsides before them. It wasn't until Sophia consulted with the map again that she realized that these were the very rounded hillsides Grandpa Yosef specified in his drawing.

"Look! Look here!" Sophia called to the sisters.

"I think my feet are cut," the younger sister huffed. "Is that dried blood between my toes?"

Her older sister helped her down a steep edge. "I

wonder if any of this traveling was worth it."

Sophia propped the sisters in front of the slopes and rested her arms over their shoulders. "You are now looking over the highland between Syria and Lebanon."

"Really!"

"You mean it?"

Sophia nodded, her lips curved into a soft smile. She lifted her eyes heavenward. At that moment, they didn't need warmth or words or anything but their hope, which they held tightly in their silence.

"We still need the darkness on our side," Sophia said, folding up the map and slipping it into her *sefer*. "We should keep going."

Hand over hand they descended the mountain, their limbs shaking from exhaustion. Sophia wiped her brow from the sandy grime that covered it. At a certain point, she shed her *chador* and veil to ward off any suspicions of a Muslim woman traveling with two non-Muslim girls.

The sun rose over the Bekaa Valley as they journeyed west past an old Syrian military base.

"We're in Lebanon," Sophia whispered.

"How can you tell?" the older sister asked.

Sophia pointed to the stronghold in the middle of the pasture. "There are the ruins of Anjar, the Armenian village which is in Lebanon."

Both sisters looked questioningly at Sophia, who grinned in response.

"Remember? Ninth grade history."

The older sister grabbed Sophia's arm. "What is next?"

Sophia shrugged. "We are in Lebanon. Next stop is Beirut, Lebanon's capital city. And after that … it's the Aretz!"

A dreamy look covered the three girls' faces. Then the older sister spoke up. "Now we're supposed to go to the rabbi of the synagogue in Beirut, right?"

"But how will we? They took everything from us," the younger sister pointed out.

"I should have thought of that," the older sister said. "We can't even pay for a bus ticket."

Sophia reached into her shoe and pulled out a few folded liras. "I have—"

"You don't!" one sister screamed. "That is amazing!" The other one leaped into the air. Both sisters jumped on Sophia and hugged her.

"Alright, that's enough." Sophia laughed. "We don't want anyone to be suspicious. Now follow me as if we belong here, as if we are all going to pick jasmine for our mothers…"

★   ★   ★

They tried to hail a cab on the road, but no one would stop for them.

The older sister held up her hand. "We can't stay out here forever."

The younger sister adjusted her shoe. "What if someone sees us?"

"Then they'll take us back to Damascus," the older sister warned.

Just the mention of it curdled Sophia's blood. "The cabbies don't want to bother with us because they think we have no money." Sophia pulled out a few liras and waved it at the next driver going by. The car came to a screeching halt. Sophia pulled open the car door and called out a price for the ride to Beirut. The cab driver nodded.

The driver let them out in Beirut's busy marketplace, where savvy merchants heckled over their wares.

Beirut ran like a free city, although the Syrian army's presence hovered over them. Muslims in Beirut received support from the Syrian government to fight among their own Christian neighbors. It was 1974 – the peak of Russia's supply of arms to Syria.

They crossed the street. An American couple passed them, followed by an Indian student and an Egyptian businessman. Everyone spoke French, validating Beirut's claim of being a "Little Paris". Sophia had to stop herself from staring at the elderly couple smoking outside a café as if on vacation. After all the stress she'd just undergone, it was hard to believe people still lived carefree and relaxed lives.

Yet she knew the *Mukhabarat* was in Beirut. She could feel them as plainly as the blisters on her feet. Was it the man in plainclothes observing the busy street from outside the café? Maybe it was the woman emptying fish guts into the street. She looked just like Huda.

Sophia elbowed the others. "We have to get to the Jewish Quarter."

"Who do we ask for directions?" the older sister pressed.

The younger sister looked sideways. "I feel like everyone is looking at us funny."

"You're right," Sophia said. "Let's split up and ask directions separately. Just make sure you only approach a Jew." She glanced around. "I can feel the *Mukhabarat* looking over my shoulder."

"Me too." The sisters trembled in unison before each walked off to inquire for directions.

Sophia pulled out a coin and picked an apricot off a cart nearby. "Where do the Jews live?" she asked the seller while she handed him her coin. He nodded toward the storefront. "Down that way."

Sudden gunfire broke out across the street. Sophia ducked behind the fruit cart. Muslims in fatigues with Palestinian rifles covered the street while shooting behind at an oncoming Christian gang. The fruit seller merely pulled a hard construction hat over his head, as if already used to the Muslim community's daily provoking of its Christian neighbors.

Within minutes, the Muslim soldiers had seized the area. They rounded up everyone who covered the busy streets. Innocent civilians surrendered, huddling with their arms above their heads. The leader of the militia scrutinized the line of people brought before him in search of Christian sympathizers or Muslim betrayers. These he threw into the hands of his militia, while the others he shoved aside with his rifle to freedom.

The head of the militia looked up to assess the next person in line. It was Sophia.

31

The head of the militia seemed to hesitate for a moment before pointing her to freedom. Sophia could not run away fast enough. Sirens sounded in the streets. The military sent in reinforcements to squash the militia, even though it was the military who had supplied the militia with Palestinian arms in the first place. She did turn around now and then, being so accustomed to traveling with the sisters. She hoped they had made it. One hopeful thought stuck in her mind; the sisters were not in the group seized by the militia when she had been pointed to freedom.

There was a Jewish woman ahead, informing her children to run to the *k'nees*. Sophia followed them through the crowds. Green banners from the Palestinian Liberation Organization waved mightily in the streets. The PLO had found its new home in Beirut and Southern Lebanon after

King Hussein had evicted them from Jordan only four years earlier. They vowed to continue with their cause in freeing Palestine of its Jews and violated every agreement with the Lebanese in the process, including regulating the activities of the Palestinian organizations.

In the valley of Abu Jamil, nothing in the landscape assisted in camouflaging people as they entered the Magen Abraham Synagogue. Men lingered within the high walls of the courtyard before they streamed down the road on their way home from morning prayers.

The rabbi there welcomed Sophia warmly and offered her something to drink. "Who is your father?"

"Shlomo Zalta."

"From Damascus?"

Sophia nodded, a lump forming in her throat at the mention of her father's name.

"It is not easy to leave your family. This is probably a most difficult thing for you, and a most tiring thing, as well. Now you will have time to rest."

The rabbi placed her in the home of an elderly couple named Mr. and Mrs. Anzarouth. "This is where you will stay until the next boat arrives from the Aretz. That is the boat on which you will travel to the Aretz. It could be tomorrow, or it could be in a few months from now. There's no way to know," he said to her. "Stay in the house, away from suspicion. Be available to leave at any time."

"Thank you."

The rabbi's parting words rang in her ears as she left him to go to the Anzarouths' home: "Don't forget; trust no one and do not leave the house."

As soon as she was inside the small house, Sophia closed the bedroom window shade that faced the street.

"You can use whatever belongings you find in the room," Mrs. Anzarouth told her. "They belonged to my daughter, may she rest in peace. I didn't have the heart to give them away."

Sophia opened the dresser drawer and found a few dresses there. At least she'd have some extra clothes to change into. She tucked Grandpa Yosef's Tehillim into a dress and closed the drawer. In the first moments of quiet, her mind drifted to Grandpa Yosef, her parents, her sister, Jack and the baby, and to every memory of her home. Deliberately, she snapped them out of her mind and replaced them with the vision of what her brothers in the Aretz had grown to look like. With that thought, she lay down on the bed and fell asleep.

The next two weeks at the older couple's home passed uneventfully. Sophia never left the house, as she had been warned, for her own safety. She did pull back the curtain now and then to rejuvenate her thoughts with life outside the four walls of the confining space she was in.

Tourism painted the streets, as Beirut convinced the world that it was much more cosmopolitan than its neighboring countries. At the same time, though, the French sign on the store across the street came down, as all foreign-named businesses were "advised" to take on Arabic names for their own good. Yes, everything seemed uneventful – until the day the search for a competent midwife reached Sophia.

An expectant woman down the block, in a sudden

panic, refused to go to the hospital, even though it was clear that her labor had begun. Her mother, having somehow found out about Sophia and the work she had done in Damascus, came running to the Anzarouths' home, begging Sophia to come help her daughter.

"You mustn't leave," Mrs. Anzarouth told Sophia. "The rabbi was very clear. Word from him could come at any minute, and you must be prepared."

Sophia slipped a shawl over her shoulders. "This is a matter of life and death."

"Yes," Mr. Anzarouth said. "Your life and your d—"

"For your own good, child," Mrs. Anzarouth pleaded, "Wait here, like the rabbi said."

"I won't be long." Sophia gave Mrs. Anzarouth a kiss on the cheek. "Don't worry about me."

Sophia tossed her shawl onto a nearby chair as soon as she walked in to the laboring woman's home. She studied the patient, then turned to the woman's mother. "Get me linens and boiled water, please. We are going to have this baby right here."

The hours passed until finally, the baby was born. Life revisited Sophia once again. Without any assistance, she had delivered a baby, acquiring the strength and the merit that belongs to anyone who accomplishes truly for the sake of another person.

When the baby's cries softened, she heard a knock at the door. It didn't frighten her. She knew who it was even before they came to tell her. "It is time, Sophia," she whispered to herself.

✶　✶　✶

In accordance with Mr. Anzarouth's instructions, Sophia entered the synagogue through a doorway inscribed with the words *ezrat nashim*. Her stomach muscles tightened as she followed the metal steps that led to a room in the cellar of the Magen Abraham Synagogue.

A crowd of about thirty people filled the room. Sophia quickly scanned the faces. The sisters with whom she had escaped Syria were there, and they immediately ran up to her, exclaiming, "You made it!"

"We stayed by our aunt ... and we never had a chance to thank you for, you know," the older sister said.

Sophia hugged them. "I know." She pulled back her soft and wavy hair in an attempt to look more presentable, although her natural beauty was evident regardless.

The rabbi who had placed her at the Anzarouths just a month earlier approached her with a plate of *ka'ak* and cheese. "Please take some before the boat arrives," he said.

"Thank you." Sophia took a *ka'ak* from the plate.

"Word from the Aretz tells us that the boat will be here tonight. We are all trying to wait patiently. All I can offer you is a seat before they come." The rabbi tapped on the chair and smiled. "Hashem be with you." Then he marched toward the corner where a girl had just set down her valises. "No belongings," the rabbi said. "We have strict rules to follow."

"What will I do with all of my things?" the girl asked, her face escaping any light because of her widely brimmed hat.

"I told you they would say that," her brother sitting beside her teased.

"Oh, really?" the girl answered him. She snapped opened one of her bags and tossed four sweaters at him. "I'm not about to leave any of my good things behind. You'll just have to wear them."

Hours later, the door opened. Three men walked in wearing silk suits and shiny shoes. It was one o'clock in the morning. The room fell silent.

One of the men circulated through the crowd, handing out pills to everyone. Sophia watched him approach her. "Take this medicine," he said to her. He could not have been older than twenty-five.

"Who are you?" she asked.

"That is not important," he said. "The medicine will stop you from becoming sick on the boat. Make sure you take it."

She sat down and placed the small pill on the table. She picked it up and then pushed it away, looking over her shoulder at some boys who were arguing over whether or not they were going to leave their valuables behind.

"Just take it," the agent mumbled. "It will make your trip much more pleasant."

Sophia edged the pill on the back of her tongue and swallowed.

The younger sister squirmed. "I hate pills."

The older sister went over to the rabbi. "When does the next boat arrive, should one miss this one?"

The rabbi smiled. "This is the last one for you and for everyone in this room."

"What if I want to go back to my family?"

"They will surely hang you if you do," one of the

agents told her.

Sophia closed her eyes and tried to think of a picture of her family. She could see them all before her, crying at her departure. Tears trickled down her face. She had created her own loss. Her father had given her a choice. She had chosen to give it all up.

The back door opened. "Quick!" an agent called out. "We will walk together, and *only* together."

Everyone lined up at the door. Only the rabbi stayed behind. Sophia turned, noting the space between the crowd and the rabbi. The crowd began to move, widening the gap.

"Walk! Now!" the agent commanded.

She walked suddenly with a force she had always known – her own will that had gotten her this far. She recognized it and let it take over again. She reminded herself of her deep intention to grow with happiness and serve Hashem in a place where her strengths could be best cultivated – so she could be the best Sophia Zalta and no one else. She remembered her dream she had fallen asleep to each night, and a smile broke out on her face. Her fears subsided. She had found comfort and familiarity.

32

"We will approach the boat in groups," an agent announced. He pointed to the boy who wore his sister's clothing piled over his small shoulders. "Everyone on line until this boy, come with me! Everyone else, wait for me to come back for you. No one moves from this hallway."

A group of ten people left with the agent.

The life Sophia had lived up until then seemed so insignificant compared to the reality now set before her. She imagined her family once again: Boomeh, rocking her baby Aharon after a midnight feeding; Jack, sleeping nearby; her father, working the night shift at a northern gas line; her mother, probably up, worrying about them all; and her grandfather, just awakening for his night-time learning.

What of Eva, to whom she never had a chance to say

good-bye or to ask if Benny finally proposed? Or of Huda, who stood out like a thorn at their sides? Would she ever hear from them again?

The same agent burst through the door. "Next group!" he called, and the second group of ten followed him out the door.

Finally, he returned for the last shift. "Everyone here! Move quickly."

Sophia filed out the door with the last of the group's members. In darkness they approached the boat. Black water glistened at the shore. Newness and uncertainty replaced her feelings of loss.

The waters flipped onto the coast of Lebanon, erasing all traces in the sand from the day. Soon their footsteps would be erased as well, once the tide rose and the waves smacked against the boulders that ran along the shore.

A small motorized raft awaited them in the shallow water, bobbing over the swells. A wave splashed over Sophia's shoe and soaked the bottom of her dress. She dipped her hand into the water just before she climbed onto the raft, rubbed her hands together, and patted her face. The salty water stung her cheeks, refreshing her.

The agent they'd been following pulled the raft over a wave and jumped in once it floated. He steered the raft into the darkness. Sophia held her breath along with those around her. No one expressed their prayers out loud, yet she felt them all nonetheless, each one's hopes running deeper than the waters they had just entered.

Soon, the raft found its way to a submarine barely surfaced in the middle of the sea. Sophia stepped up into the submarine, drawing in the moist air scented with the promises of an open sea.

"Another person is on the shore!" one of the agents called down to the captain. He peered through his binoculars one more time. "The rabbi is with him. We are sending the raft out one more time!"

"It's too risky!" the captain answered back on his hand-held radio. "We've been out here long enough!"

"We can't leave him there. It might be more dangerous for all of us." The agent jumped back into the motorized raft.

When the raft came in with its passenger, the captain sealed the submarine's lid behind them. "This is it," he called out.

The last of the escapees bent down into the small compartment. The first thing Sophia noticed about him was the way he descended the steps into the submarine - in one continuous motion.

She stepped across the railing inside the boat, behind the row of passengers. A light from inside the submarine lit up his profile. It was him. It had to be him.

He looked up at the crowd of people and scanned the faces until he spotted hers. He bowed his head gently in her direction.

Sophia still recognized his way and it gave her reassurance. She could not formulate her words into a proper introduction. "Matlub?" she said.

"Timing is everything," he answered her.

"What are you doing here?" she asked.

"I was going to ask you the same question."

"My father woke me in the middle of the night. A Bedouin girl had passed away. Our descriptions were similar."

"So it all worked out, and you were able to leave Damascus after all."

"You don't look surprised."

Matlub inched forward. "It's not every day that a girl with your description dies of typhoid."

A chord struck inside her. She gripped the railing, suddenly cognizant of the diving submarine. "I never said that she had typhoid."

He rubbed his cheek and smiled. "I saw your father paying Huda's hospital bill. He asked me to contact him if I knew of any bodies that ... fit your description."

Sophia shook her head in disbelief. "You mean - it was you?"

"Actually, it was you. Your father told me about your idea, which was quite ingenious, if I may say so. Later, I called him in to identify the body of a Bedouin as his daughter."

Sophia shook her head again. "I thought you had left ... disappeared."

"I had for a little bit, but I came back."

"I knew I saw you in the hospital," she said, "but I still don't understand. Why did you leave? And what was it that made you come back?"

Matlub took a step back. "I thought about how much you wanted to leave Damascus. I wanted to continue seeing you, but at the same time, I didn't want to hold you back from following your dream. So I stayed out of sight for a while – for your sake, to give you the chance to escape. Once I found out your plan of escape, though, I knew it was time for me to come out of hiding."

The submarine descended to an undetected depth.

His voice went low. "And now that I have followed you all the way here, Sophia, I should tell you—"

She had too much intuition to look his way.

"The reason I am on this boat is because of you. I am asking you to be my wife."

Complete joy overcame her, and for a moment, she couldn't speak.

"I also promised your father that I would take care of his … his …"

Sophia looked into the eyes of the man she would soon marry until the word popped into her head. "*Musawi?*" she said, rescuing him.

Glossary_____

Abalek (A)	*lit. by you, in the future*
Amid (A)	An official of the secret police as in captain or corporal
Araq (A)	A clear, anise-flavored, distilled alcoholic beverage
Argilah (A)	A water pipe with a flexible tube for smoking tobacco
Bameh (A)	Okra in tomato sauce
Beje'nen (A)	*lit. to make you crazy;* unbelievable
Bisid (A)	Roasted seeds
Bizeh b'jurah (A)	Green peas, rice, and meat spiced with coriander
Brit milah (H)	Circumcision
Chador (A)	A cloak thrown over the head and closed in the front
Chalas (A)	Over, done
Chupah (H)	*lit. wedding canopy;* marriage ceremony

Dallal (A)	Matchmaker
Dallaleh (A)	Female matchmaker
Ejjeh (A)	Fried egg pancake with a variety of combinations such as meat, vegetables, or cheese
Ejjeh bakdounez (A)	Fried parsley-and-onion pancake laced with allspice
Ejjeh lahmeh (A)	Fried meat pancake laced with allspice and cinnamon
Ezrat nashim(H)	Ladies courtyard
Haret (A)	Neighborhood
Haret-al-Yahud (A)	The Jewish Quarter
Hohsh(A)	A residence with an outdoor courtyard, usually walled on all sides
Imshe yulla (A)	Move on already
Ka'ak (A)	Crunchy, roped pastry bracelets mostly flavored with aniseed and sprinkled with sesame seeds
Katayif (A)	Sweet pancake-like pastries that are filled and then baked or fried and drizzled with sugar syrup
Keftes(A)	Saucy meatballs
K'nees (A)	Synagogue
Kibbe (A)	A fried torpedo made of cracked wheat and stuffed with meat
Lebas (A)	Sugar-coated almonds
Labneh (A)	Yogurt spread
Mabruk (A)	*lit. Should be blessed;* An expression for "congratulations" or "good luck"
Mazal (H)	Fortune; luck
Mazza (A)	Appetizers
Mishnah (H)	The Oral Torah

Mukhabarat (A)	Secret Police
Musawi (A)	Follower of Moshe
Naseeb (A)	Soul-mate
Oud (A)	A pear-shaped stringed instrument commonly used in Middle Eastern music
Pidyon ha'ben (H)	The redeeming of a first-born son by a Kohen
Sefer Tehillim (H)	The Book of Psalms
Semboosak (A)	Half moon pastries stuffed with either meat or cheese
Shlonek (A)	How are you?
Shraab-il-lohz (A)	Sweet almond milk
Sefer (H)	Book
Sham (A)	An ancient name for Damascus
Shamosh (H)	Caretaker of a synagogue
Souk (A)	A covered marketplace
Succah (H)	Booth for temporary living outside
Ta'amim (H)	Cantillations
Tallit (H)	Prayer shawl
Tarboosh (A)	Conical hat
Toleh (A)	Backgammon

Key:	A= Arabic; H= Hebrew